PSYCHOBITCHES

TEAR IT UP

JAMIE HAWKE

D1714464

DOUBLE DOWN PRESS

Editors
Diane Newton
Tracey Byrnes

PSYCHOBITCHES: TEAR IT UP (this book) is a work of
fiction.

All of the characters, organizations, and events portrayed in this
novel are either products of the author's imagination or are used
fictitiously. Sometimes both.

WELCOME

Want a FREE Book? I have a fun little "Guide to Building Your Harem" from the Planet Kill world hat I will be sharing via the newsletter. Get them by signing up:

SIGN UP HERE

WARNING: This book contains gratuitous violence and sex, harems, and crazy amounts of superpowered fun. If you enjoy all that, read on! Otherwise… run like crazy.

If you'd like to keep updated on new stories, freebies, and recommendations of other stories I admire, come check out my FaceBook page at:

https://www.facebook.com/JamieHawkeAuthor.

Thank you for reading!

All the best,

Jamie Hawke

There's nothing wrong with psychos, especially when capturing the supervillain variety means filling my bank account with credits. Hell, even better when they look like Erupa—full lips, tight ass, and cleavage that could make a man weep. Hot as fuck. You know, minus the horns. Some would point to her blue skin as a negative, but it kinda worked for me.

What gets me though is when one of those damn psycho chicks tries to blow my brains out with titty-guns or leaves a mine on my seat, right where it would blow my nuts off. That was the story of capturing Cheri only yesterday, but now she was locked up and I had to deal with this crazy *chica* as my last stop before heading on to deposit them in the loony bin on Abaddon.

Oh, and in case you were wondering—I managed to retain my nuts. All in a day's work for a man of the law... kinda. Technically, I'm a bounty hunter, but where I'm from the words are semi-interchangeable. When people speak of Ezra Faldron, criminals cower. I wore the word "Police" because I fucking brought the law.

At that moment, it wasn't exactly proving easy.

Erupa is basically of the demon type of supervillains. Not a demon, exactly, but due to the effects of our sun, Oram, and how it mutated the humans who colonized its system long ago, various supers developed powers. I'm not sure if it was due to blood type or something else in our genes, but many developed similar powers and mutated in similar ways. You have your normal-looking humans like me, some animal-looking ones like the famed criminal Charm, and then there are the demon ladies like Erupa. Some have horns permanently, others can grow and retract them.

All very fascinating, right? Considering the fact that she'd just pinned my arm to the wall with her fucking horns as we struggled, they were first and foremost in my mind.

Erupa let out a scream of frustration as she tried to dig her nails into my jugular— long and sharp nails, basically claws—while I had my free arm pressing down on her forearm, hand on her other horn to try and wrench her free.

"I'm not going to that hell, you motherfucker!" she grunted as I wrenched her horns away. One good elbow to the face and then a push-kick sent her falling back, but she was stronger and faster than me, so recovered and came back with a series of strikes. While she was quick, I'd spent my youth on the planet known as Xian training my body and mind. A mind that, in fights like these would sometimes help because of my empath powers. But when everything was in full-on aggression mode, all I got was a sense that my opponent wanted me to die, which feels more like common sense than anything super. Still, my training helped me anticipate blows based on body movement, and block them based on muscle memory and instinct.

A slash of claws came for my face and I blocked from the outside, landing a blow on her ribs that sent her stumbling back. When she looked up, her eyes were glowing red as a similar glow formed from her hand, smoke trailing up and toward me.

Damn. I must've let my SupraTech Quencher lapse. Hitting the button on the square device at my side, I grinned as the glow vanished from her hand just as she pushed out, leaving her staring at me in frustration. Part of being a bounty hunter for the

Orion Corporation meant being able to gain access to the rarest forms of supra tech, or items that had been infused with stolen superpowers. One of the top hunters for Orion Corp, a legendary super named Ranger, had led the effort and was off continuing to build the company's supply of energy and powers. In a way, he was a god among supers, and all of us hunters hoped to meet him one day.

"That's cheating," Erupa growled. "Where's the honor?"

"You don't get to speak to me about honor," I spat back. "Not after all the innocent blood you've spilled."

"Define innocent," she said, then charged. Only, before reaching me, she jumped and pushed off of the stone pillar to my left, propelling herself in the opposite direction, over the counter, and toward the door.

She was running!

"Dammit!" I shouted, taking off after her. My hand instinctively went to my pistol, but no, that was certain death for her. In this case, death wasn't on the table—not if I wanted to get paid. Plus, that always ruined the excitement of the hunt.

I charged after her, slamming through the doors and out into the street of this swampy planet with its vine-covered domes, bars and whorehouses, places assassins like her would congregate in. The number of contracts I could likely grab here would pay me for years, but this was always more than contracts for me. This was about getting the really nasty ones. And there was the fact that my ship was about full, once I captured her.

She was charging down the street, nearly out of range of my Quencher, and I considered shooting for her legs. A large man slammed into my side, picking me up and tackling me into the cliff face that much of the town had been built against. He was vaguely familiar, likely someone with a contract out on him who assumed I'd come for him. No time for assholes—I broke his grip with two arms down on his and a knee to the crotch then blasted him back with a surge of electricity from my arc baton.

Scanning for Erupa, a hint of doubt crept in. Had I lost her? She was out of my range by now, and that meant—the shadows! I sprinted in the direction I'd last seen her, looking for any sign of ripples in the darkness near others. There were only two people on the streets, both Santoori whores, women known for giving you the worst kinds of pain combined with the best types of pleasure. Not my thing in the slightest, but I wasn't looking at them for their skills in bed, but to see where Erupa would resurface. The one directly ahead seemed like she would have been too easy a choice, so I turned left, going for the other. Sure enough, Erupa had materialized behind her and, seeing my approach, cursed. She shoved the whore my way and took off running again.

"Don't make me!" I shouted, hand on my pistol and growling in annoyance.

She was strong, but I was faster. From what I'd heard about her power, it required a cool-down time, which meant she couldn't use it again immediately. So I moved my hand away from the pistol and put my full energy into my sprint. She was mine.

I chased after her until we got to the next corner, and then I plowed into her, the two of us going right through a wall. It broke and splintered as we landed on a large, circular bed and screams filled the night as nude women sprang up around us, running for safety. A man with an erection lay there, a piece of splintered wood stuck into his leg. He yelped as he shouted, "Oh yeah, keep it going," before realizing this wasn't part of the famed Santoori system and that he was actually bleeding.

"My apologies," I said, pressing Erupa to the bed as I bound her arms behind her.

"What the fuck is this?" the madam of the house shouted, charging in to see the broken wall.

Meanwhile, the man was staring at his blood seeping out onto the bed and starting to hyperventilate.

"Finish him off and consider yourself lucky I don't bring in your whole clientele," I replied, then did a quick scan of her. Not worth much in the bounty hunter trade, but she had a price on her head. Seeing me and the words police across my chest, she took a step back, motioned to her women, and walked off.

As I pulled Erupa up and stuck her with a needle that would pacify her long enough to get her out of there, three women went back to the man and started working him while one dealt with his injury. The mixture of screams and moans wasn't abnormal for this place, but that didn't stop it from giving me a creeped-out chill.

"Fuck… you," Erupa managed as she stumbled out of there with me shoving her along. "When this wears off… you're…"

The next words came out in a slur but were likely meant to be a death threat or something of the sort. "You're dead" was about as common in my line of work as my cup of coffee in the mornings. That thought got my cravings going… Maybe some Sumatran dark roast. Mmmm.

I shrugged it off because if I gave a shit every time my life was threatened, I'd be all out of shit.

And honestly, the idea of that man having his bloody orgy was still making me feel so uncomfortable and grossed-out, not much could've gotten through.

Others emerged to glare at me as we passed through town, but nobody acted. Cowards, too often concerned about their own necks to band together as a group and take me on. Good for me, at least.

Bound and gagged, I dragged Erupa onto my ship. It wasn't a large craft, but big enough for six cells, the last of which she was about to occupy. The outside was fitted with two sets of blasters on each wing and one main turret at the base, a typical Orion hunter ship with police blue and red I'd painted on. That wasn't standard, and most of the other hunters didn't embrace the law enforcement angle like me, but most of them were bastards to begin with. I wouldn't be surprised if I were hired to take in half of them in my career, at some point.

Erupa grunted, trying to say something, but I shoved her forward through the dark passage that led to the bars of the remaining cell.

"Holy fucklicks," Cheri said as we passed her cell. She stood from her toilet, panties still around her ankles but with a mini-skirt that fell to keep her as decent as could be, and grinned. "Got you a demon lay, huh big guy? Hold those horns tight when she goes down on you, in case you need to yank her back. Sharp teeth and all."

That grin spread even wider. I glared, hating some aspects of my job. While Erupa was a criminal and definitely not of your normal mindset, Cheri was batshit crazy. She wore her blue hair in pigtails and a very revealing red outfit with torn fishnet stockings. The left breast of her outfit was adorned with a cute yellow smiley face that stood out against the bright red. A heart was tattooed under her right eye, along with permanent eyeliner on each side with a vertical line that went up and down, giving her a sort of clown look. She also had a tattoo on her left arm that said "Love Stinks." When I'd taken her in, she'd fought me with a sword, which in itself wasn't crazy, but I had to wonder about the small teddy bear chained to the end of the hilt.

Another grunt came from Erupa and she pushed off as she tried to charge the cell, but I held her in place by the shackles, earning us a high-pitched cackle from Cheri.

"Oooh, feisty to boot," the crazy lady said. "Maybe I'll get a piece of her when you're done?"

"Shut the fuck up, Cheri," I said, pointing at her with my arc baton, letting electricity flow from it to show her I wasn't afraid to give her a good shock. It put the criminals in their place. Since I honestly hated having to hit them, this worked as a last resort.

Cheri's grin faded and she flipped up her skirt as she turned away, giving us a nice view of the moon. With a sigh, I pushed Erupa on. The others were either sleeping or not caring to get involved. They knew their fate was sealed. When we arrived at the third cell over, I opened it with a hand scan and shoved her in.

"For the record," I said, as the gate slid shut, "I'm not like that. Any cop who takes advantage of their prisoners deserves to be put behind bars with the rest of you."

I gestured her forward and removed her gag.

"Then I know a lot of *cops* who need to be put in their place," Erupa said as she worked her jaw and turned to have her restraints off. "Tell you what, I'll make a trade. You let me go, I'll give you all the names of every dirty, rotten hunter out there."

"Not happening," I said, already walking away. "And you'll get your restraints off when we're airborne. Nothing personal, just have to make sure we're out of here without any problems first."

A couple of hushed curses followed me, but nothing further. That was more than I could say for the others. Brock in cell six still had marks from the bars on his face when he tried headbutting his way out, and Cheri had nearly dislocated a shoulder trying to fit through the bars. It never would've worked, but she did manage to get one shoulder and a boob through before yelping in pain and requiring my assistance to get back through. Ever had to shove a tit through prison bars? Awkward, to say the least.

I'd since decided to activate the electricity on the bars, though I hated to. Every once in a while I'd get a real whackjob who wouldn't let up, regardless, and the whole ship would smell of burnt flesh by the time it was over. Plus, arriving with dead or even nearly dead cargo didn't pay nearly half as well. Especially now, according to the charts I'd seen come in through the comms.

Reason being? Apparently, they were going to start a new program, one where they would introduce some of the more adept criminals into the system on the other side of the planet—a contained reality show, in a sense. While I dealt with capturing supers and delivering them to a no-powers-allowed facility, the planet boasted various uses for these criminals. Worst of which was a black market show not available to supers, but apparently broadcast to sick Earthers and their type.

Supers like Erupa would never be sent into that mess because of their looks—humans in the Milky Way weren't supposed to know such mutations existed. There were those who were aware, but the majority of them had been fed a line of propaganda that they were all that existed in the universe.

Were there more than them and us supers? We were, after all, merely humans who had been changed in the many years since colonizing Oram's system. I had no idea if there could be more out there, but if they were so ignorant of us, I had to wonder what I, in turn, might be unaware of.

Cheri would most likely be one of those sent out to fight in Abaddon, so she was worth a pretty penny. Erupa would likely be treated in the insane asylum, kept there for testing. Both would be sucked dry of their powers, left as husks of their former selves, and their powers would be used for making new supra tech. That is unless they could be somehow convinced to join Ranger's army and work for Orion Corp. It happened, the rumors said.

And then there was my newest pet, a recent capture who I wasn't sure I wanted to give up. A super who could change size from large to small and back again, I'd caught her with the Quencher when in small form, and that's how she was now.

I kept her in a little lantern next to the controls in the cockpit. Her real supervillain name had been Flyer, but that sounded stupid. I'd decided to call her Tink, based on an old story that had been passed down through generations, kept alive by the earliest settlers from Earth. She had the wings and all, and truly hated being referred to as a fairy. But hey, what fun was there in capturing ruthless killers if you couldn't antagonize them while debating their fates?

Entering the cockpit, I tapped on the glass to wake her up and shrugged at her glare. "All ready to make the delivery. I thought you'd like to know."

"Eat me," she said groggily from where she lay curled up on the bottom of the glass.

"As much as I could actually do that, sorry, fairies don't sit well in my stomach."

That woke her up, and she flew at the glass, punching it twice before stopping to hold her fist in pain. When her powers were working, she maintained her regular strength even when small. Thanks to my Quencher and the backup on board, that wasn't the case at that moment.

"Fuck you," she said.

"Real creative. I thought fairies were supposed to be mischievous. Shouldn't you have some better insults in you?"

This time she sat back down, folding her legs up to her chest, and ignored me.

"Suit yourself," I said, bringing the ship to life with a roar. "It's going to be a boring flight if you don't want to chat though."

Silence.

With a sigh, I took off, shaking my head as I wondered for the hundredth time why I'd gotten into this line of work. Of course, it was for the sense of duty I felt, wanting to be part of Orion Corp, to one day live up to legends like Ranger and the others. There was the payday, sure, but it was more than money for me.

If I made this delivery, I might get the chance I'd been looking for—a chance to go on a mission with Ranger, to truly make a difference on the front lines.

All I had to do was keep my eyes open, my wits about me. Get in, deliver the prisoners, and get out. I was determined not to let anything go wrong because it was my time to shine.

Boy, was I in for a rude awakening.

2

We entered Abaddon's atmosphere early the next night, and I immediately had to activate shields to protect the ship from one of the planet's many acid rain storms. We'd entered too far off course, and the fields of Abaddon's combat show passed far below. Once we were through what some called "The Chaos Zone," the acid rains and whatnot wouldn't be a problem. I glanced down, feeling almost sorry for the poor devils who ended up in that hellhole.

What would they be doing right now to escape the storm? Either they'd be eaten alive by the acid, or had retreated to the old bunkers and tunnels that had been set up to keep out the drainage, I supposed.

And when confined like that, the killings likely got worse.

Our destination, however, was the asylum compound. It was completely separated from the rest by a no man's land, then guard outposts and other defenses. I pushed the ship to the max, not wanting to take on any more risk than I needed to, and was glad to see the mountains that soon showed on the other side of no man's land.

"Welcome to your new home, Tink," I said.

"Maybe you should come down with us, stay for a while," she shot back with a grin. "Could give you a tour…"

I laughed. "In and out, that's my motto."

"Ah, that type of guy." She came toward the glass, pressing her tiny ass against it as if that would do anything. "Come on, minute man. Let's see what you've got."

"First of all, you're not my type. Second, you do realize you're about the size of my dick, right?"

She scoffed. "Doubt it. And if you let me change to full size, we'd be having a different discussion right now."

I shook my head. "Ain't gonna happen."

With a pout, she sat down again. We watched the mountain grow larger, seconds later passing over it. I thought I saw a glow on the hills and several people, alerting my internal alarm. But when I glanced back and then ran a quick scan with my ship's hunter ability, it showed nobody there.

Good, because this place had strict rules about who could be where, and people on the mountain, as far as I could figure, could only mean an attempted escape. Whether that would be the psychos trying to break out and make a run for the Chaos Zone or vice versa, it would be equally stupid.

Trying to take down my ship so that they could steal it and get out of there would be another matter entirely, so I had to be extra cautious.

"You have this look on your face," Tink said.

"Oh?"

"Like there's a little turd sticking out of your butt and it won't exit or go back in. A hard one, maybe stinging a bit from too many jalapenos. Is that the case, big guy?" She looked up at me innocently, batting her eyelashes.

"You sure have a huge mouth for such a little lady."

"I'll take that as a yes." She laughed, though it didn't do a good job of hiding the fear she had to be feeling at coming to a place like this.

"What made you do it?" I asked.

"Do what?"

I shrugged. "Whatever it is you did to end up here."

"You're fucking serious right now?" She stood, hands against the glass. "Are you telling me you brought me in, and don't even know what for?"

"Listen, fairy, I have a job to do. I do my job. That's it."

She shook her head like a disappointed mom. "Assassination."

"You assassinated someone?"

She nodded, proud. "That's right. Shrunk like this, flew in through the window, and managed to get some poison into this fuck's morning coffee. Two sips and he finally sets down his tablet, looks at me sitting there, smiling, and then falls over dead. If I hadn't been so cocky, I would've gotten out of there. But the fucker hit a silent alarm as he was falling, and the whole place went into lockdown mode, metal shutters sliding down over the windows and all. Imagine, little ol' me being trapped like that. I flipped, beating the shit out of him as I tried to find a way to turn off the alarms and all that. If it were just the poison, I could've gotten away with it—hid or something until the responders opened up the place. Unfortunately, as small as I can get, my temper is always fifty times too big. They found me, fists covered in blood."

"But... I caught you."

"Yeah, but only after I killed all of them too, and got away. Why do you think I was in the system?"

"Fuck," I replied, shaking my head. "Sometimes I'd rather not know this stuff."

"They were all bad people. Like yourself."

"I'm on the side of the law," I corrected her.

"Ah, but that's the kicker, isn't it... Whose law?"

My brow furrowed and I glanced around for headphones or anything to tune her out, instead opting for music. Some people like to ride into victory with crazy metal or punk from the old days, for others, it's new wave intensity shit. Me? I blared a mixture of classical violin and opera because I was a fucking gentleman. Sure, my job required me to slam a woman's face into the pavement from time to time, but only hardened criminals who'd killed and maimed innocents. When it came to helping the elderly cross the road or holding a door open for a woman, I was your man. A child lost and crying? I'd find the parents.

And when I listened to music, I did it like a champion. Joining in without knowing the words this guy was singing or even understanding the language, my baritone voice told the world I was in charge and about to rise to the position in life I'd been meant for.

"Fucking kill me now!" Tink was shouting in her squeaky little voice, but I ignored her and kept on singing as I brought the ship in for a landing.

We were past the main defenses now, in the landing yard just outside of the main compound. Through the window, we could make it out in the darkness: a tall, thick cement wall with iron gates, and past it a building that resembled a castle with towers at each corner, battlements in between and even arrow slits along the walls. Those were just the extra defenses, though, as I knew the inside was like any other testing and treatment facility. Long hallways with reinforced steel on all doors, padded rooms for the real crazy ones, and doctors equipped with stun batons in case the situation got out of hand.

"Seriously," Tink said, voice now trembling. "I'll suck your tiny cock right now, just… let the jar fall, turn a blind eye while I escape. I can do it shrunken or big, either way."

The number of times sexual favors had been offered in exchange for freedom was too numerous to count—from both male and female captives—and this time didn't make me consider it any more than the others. Was she hot when normal size? Hell yes, but many supers were. It was something with the genes, maybe the effects of Oram or perhaps it had something to do with the original colonists. I don't know, but to be hot among our kind was all relative. I knew this because I'd been one of the rare supers who had been to Abaddon aside from the criminals, and I'd seen some of the crazies they unleashed in the Chaos Zone—supers and Earthers. To say there was a genetic difference was an understatement.

Hell, with the way I ate there was no way I'd have had the six-pack I did if it wasn't for being a super.

"Come on, man," Tink went on as if I was even considering it. "Imagine my little tongue, maybe I turn around and flutter my wings against your balls, we—"

"Tink, shut it. Ain't gonna happen."

"Let me out of here you fucking ogre! You tiny-dick mother bitch! Let me the fuck out!"

I glanced down, somewhere between humored and annoyed, and shook my head. "Here I was thinking we could be friends someday if they ever let you free. Do friends talk like that to each other?"

She glared, gestured sucking me off, and then pretended to bite the imaginary dick in her mouth before spitting it on the floor. "One of these days, asshole. You'll get yours."

I shook my head, ignoring her to focus on the

landing. We were here, and it was time to be rid of this load so I could get on with my life. Another day, another huge disc full of credits.

I soon had them all in a line at the top of the ramp as it opened, chained with shock capacity engaged. Tink was still in the lantern in my hand, earning us curious glances from the others. There weren't many supers who could change size like she could, and I imagined they were more than a little impressed with the fact that I'd captured her. A man approached to make the payment, so I gestured them forward, but the large bastard in the front went too fast and caused the others to stumble.

Cheri let out a yelp as she tripped, the chain twisting so that I had to leap forward and catch her with my free arm to stop it from letting out the shock it would give her if she attempted to break free. She stared up at me with wide eyes, as if I'd saved her from the edge of the cliff.

"So you do care," Cheri said and reached out as if to caress my face. An awkward moment passed where her fingers touched my cheek, and I had no free hands to push her away. She grinned, winked, and then stood on her own. "Unfortunately for you, mister, I have a previous engagement I must be getting to."

This mock formality was almost humorous from

her, but when I heard Tink rapping on the side of the lantern's glass. I looked down and realized I'd been staring after the crazy woman.

"Yeah, thought I'd save you from that silly grin," Tink said with a cold stare, but even she had a bit of a smile. "You're still an asshole."

There was a look in her eyes that showed maybe she didn't think I was so bad after all. When I focused on her, dialing down my Quencher to test her emotions with my powers, I saw it was true. Interesting. Even Erupa was giving me an assessing glance, though she quickly turned away when she saw that I'd noticed.

All that changed when the collectors met us in the yard. Not the regular guy, I noted, but a slightly chubby guard who had an angle to his brow that made me wonder if he'd had it smashed in once and couldn't get it fixed. Another joined him, this one looking like he'd just entered the workforce, and started checking the merchandise. They gave me the chip with my credits, and I scanned it to ensure it was all there. Giving them a nod, I was about to return to my ship when an explosion sounded, followed by gunfire.

I glanced back at the ladies, making eye contact with Erupa first and then Cheri. It wasn't that I cared what happened to them, more that I was worried about my merchandise. Delivering goods only to see it destroyed immediately affects someone... and maybe I cared, too. Whatever.

Strange, I thought—the sound of the fighting was coming from the same direction I thought I'd seen people before. Not exactly, but close. Too close to be a coincidence, so I started walking briskly toward my ship. The last thing I needed was anyone accusing me of being part of whatever this was.

The fighting was picking up, a building even collapsing in the distance, from what I could tell. And then there were figures moving our way, so I started sprinting for my ship. This wasn't good.

Shouts echoed behind me, and I glanced back to see a guard fall, men and women charging out of the asylum. Guards were pulling their batons, some on the towers bringing guns into it, but it didn't make sense. How had the inmates escaped? My delivery was there, chains off, and it looked like they were about to join in the fight.

My work here was done. I thought about going back, taking sides... but Orion Corp could handle themselves. The last thing I needed was to draw attention to myself, even if I could take out as many of them as I had bullets for, and maybe a couple more.

If they caught me, I was a dead man. Their

aggressiveness tasted like spoiled wine in my mouth. With that in mind, I put everything into my sprint, determined to make it to my ship. Almost there, I actually dared to hope…

And then it blew up.

3

It was official—I was royally fucked. A large number of the inmates in this place were here because of me, and from what I could tell they were winning this coup. My ship was grounded, which meant I was too unless there were more vessels nearby.

My best bet was to charge around to the other side of the mob, where past experience had shown guard ships stashed. Even if I could get to them, though, that didn't mean I'd have access. Who knows what sort of security procedures they'd have in place, considering that they had to discourage the inmates from escaping and taking off in them.

So what then?

A shot hit the dirt nearby, and I spun to see that one of the prisoners was responsible for it. Not a single guard that I could see was still standing. Scanning the ramparts, there was no doubt the guards had lost. I could just see one remaining guard there, but already figures were charging along the top of the walls toward his location.

Whatever my next step, it couldn't be simply standing there getting shot at, so I ran. Figuring that the mob was in my path, my first instinct was survival. There had to be comms equipment and whatnot in the building. Maybe someone would already be trying to get hold of Orion Corp to call for backup. Send in the fucking cavalry!

But what if they were all taken out? No more of their guards and doctors left? Well, in that case... dammit, my brain couldn't process all this at the moment. Instead of trying there, I decided to head for the mountains. After everything calmed down, I would be able to get a better sense of what was happening and strategize before making my move, if nobody else had done so yet.

It was hard to tell how long I ran, at moments ducking behind hills, then thinking I heard others approaching—even though my powers didn't pick up on anything, they weren't exactly strong enough to be reliable in such situations. With my heart thudding and my mind spinning as I tried to think of a way to get out of there, I found a vantage point to see that there were still many going at each other in hand-to-hand combat in addition to the shots that rung out from a distance.

At least they wouldn't have their powers... yet. Many of them had been drained, but the ones they were still trying to train for service with Orion Corp could be a threat, along with any new deliveries. I had little doubt about what Tink and the others would've liked to do to me. If the inmates reached the supra tech that held their powers in check and were able to dismantle it, we could be in some serious shit.

Thinking about all of this, I realized sweat was dripping down my back and temples, and my hands were all clammy. I blinked, trying to get rid of this dizzy, foggy feeling. My breathing was coming short and forced, and I would've loved to have something to punch.

"Keep your head in the game," I hissed. Fuck, I hated losing my shit like this. But my training at the temple should have been able to help me avoid this panic. If I was truly as skilled as my *sifu* had led me to believe, none of this damn panic would've even been a worry.

I could only recall one other time that I'd experienced a panic like this, and that was the day I became a cop. Or... bounty hunter. Or whatever.

That first contract, the moment you're on the ground tracking a known supervillain... it's terrifying.

I still remember the way the leaves had parted, giving me a view of the supervillain's orange and black tails flailing out behind him. They shot out for me, each acting of their own accord like scorpion tails attached to whips. My superpower isn't like many out there. It's not that I'm super strong or fast, or that I can shoot fireballs out of my ass, as pleasant as that sounds. No, my power comes in the form of being a low-level Empath. What that means is that I'm able to feel the emotions of others, broken down on a fundamental level.

When there are a lot of others around me, it's not so useful because I can't be sure whose emotions I'm feeling. When it's one-on-one though, it can be quite effective. Imagine, for example, if someone's about to attack—do their emotions change? You bet your ass they do. In this case, the bastard's confidence sparked, as he apparently thought he had me in a trap. I lunged back, dodging the strikes, and had him with a good shot of my bolas, the two weights wrapping around so that the cord took his legs and slammed him to the ground. Thrusting myself forward, I zapped him with my arc baton. As quickly as that, he was bagged and ready for delivery.

You can imagine my powers have come into play in many ways over the years, for good or bad. It was shit when I'd have someone ready to go, knowing the evil of their ways, and then be hit with a flood of horror and sorrow as they started realizing they wouldn't see their families again, or whatever else was going through their minds.

I'd learned early on to shut it off when no longer needed.

But when people asked me what my powers were, I usually gave a simple answer—justice. Lame? Whatever, it's what I did. I brought justice and was damn good at it. So from the moment I caught that son of a bitch, I'd never felt a panic attack again—until now, that is. It had shown me what I was capable of. That if I just found the pattern, nothing could stop me except for true spontaneity. Those bastards couldn't escape me. I'd been the king of the jungle, and I wasn't about to let this bring me down now.

Thinking about how I'd come to this spot as I ran brought back my confidence, reminding me that I could get through this. I just needed to connect the dots. See the patterns in what they were doing, and maybe find someone from Orion Corp who could get me out of here. One idea was to run over to the Chaos Zone and hope a camera would spot me, warn them that I didn't belong, and they'd send someone.

But what if they didn't? Then I'd be stuck in a land of acid rain and even worse killers than here. No, that wouldn't do, so I continued to rack my mind.

At a ridge in the mountains I doubled back, but at an angle so that I could reach the far side of the asylum compound. The way I figured it, the trees back there could provide more cover, more areas for me to stay out of sight until the chaos died down.

A few paces past the first trees, though, I slowed, realizing there was an emotion out there.

Fright. Somebody nearby was feeling fright, which meant I wasn't the only one. The funny thing about fear is it can be viewed in the sense that you have nothing to worry about because the other side is afraid. But that would be wrong, nine times out of ten. Those nine times, the afraid party is more dangerous, at least when dealing with the sort of supervillains I hunted. When they were afraid, they'd do anything to stay safe. They'd flail around, let their powers get out of control, and sometimes even blow themselves up. Okay, that last one only happened once, but it was disgusting.

Imagine having to clean that shit off the inside of your ship!

My next steps came slowly, full of caution and ready for someone to come charging out, or lightning to explode out of nowhere. The place smelled of sulfur and pines, a cool breeze reminding me I hadn't been smart enough to grab my helmet when leaving the ship. One well-placed shot to the head and I'd be done for.

Whoever this guy was, his fright was close now. I crouched low, turning to try to get a sense of where exactly it was coming from. Each step brought a crunch of dried pine needles, so I was careful not to move and give myself away.

Needles crunching... Panic and fright changed to aggression. I spun, knowing the attack was coming.

And so it did, preceded by a war cry—the most idiotic thing anyone could do right before attacking because it gave everything away. I made sure to block off my emotions, lest the fear and panic take me over as well, and crouched, facing the source of that sound.

A short man in a tattered asylum outfit jumped, kicking off of a tree trunk nearby, coming at me with a much-practiced leaping kick that, unfortunately for him, wouldn't do any good against me. I'd trained too much to be caught by such simple tricks, and stepped into it, grabbing his leg, and then spun to throw him to the ground. His leg was still locked in my grip, so I stomped on his nuts, then twisted the ankle so that it snapped.

"Motherfucker!" he screamed, pounding the ground and attempting to lunge for me, but I'd seen movement on the level ground between the asylum and our position. A mob out for blood, who'd likely heard the man's scream. They could have him. I was off.

Darting between trees, I ran in the darkness. The more trees surrounding me, the less likely the mob would be able to find me in the dark, or hit me with random shots.

I skidded down underneath a fallen tree, rolled, and vaulted up and over a boulder in my path. My eyes were searching for any sort of hiding spot, as I knew I couldn't outrun these punks forever. One came flying down from the tree trunk and nearly tackled me, instead only catching my leg and causing me to almost fall.

Kicking him off, I turned to see a pistol leveled at me, but then tripped just as it went off. A foot in the guy's face got him off of me, and when I threw myself back I hadn't counted on a hill there so went tumbling.

A rock hit me in the ribs, a tree upside the head, but I continued to fall. When I came to a stop at the bottom of a small valley, two more jumped down after me while the rest were apparently moving on or waiting it out, I couldn't be sure.

There was no fear in the air, only pure aggression, and elation. They were looking forward to tearing my heart out and devouring it, no doubt.

"Fuck, back off!" I shouted, trying to push myself to my feet but stumbling and collapsing to my hands and knees. The forest floor was spinning, blotches in my vision.

"Tear his back off?" one of them said. "Gruesome, I like it."

I lunged, swinging with one hand as I tried to reach for my arc baton with my other, but the taller of the two caught me with a kick that sent me onto my back, another rock connecting with my head. The crack left a reverberating pain through my skull, and I lay there staring up at the leaves, willing myself to stand.

A *thwap* sounded, then a *crack*. Muffled shouting, another *crack* followed by a grunt, and then... silence.

My first thought was that a bear, or something worse, had just attacked them and would come for me next. I told myself to get up, but my body wouldn't respond. I took a deep breath, wanting to yell at myself, to attack my body for not responding. I didn't care how hurt and beat up it was, this was the time to react, to get up and fight or run if I wanted to survive the night.

Blue, almost turquoise pigtails. That was my first thought. Then I realized what I was looking at—or rather, who. Cheri. I was truly fucked. She was shaking her head, grinning, and I could only imagine all the thoughts going through her mind about how she would skin me alive or kill me in some other gruesome way.

Odd, then, that her emotions seemed to speak of sympathy.

Even weirder when her hand caressed my face and she asked if I could get up and walk.

"I... don't know," I replied.

"Time to fucking find out," she replied in her sing-song way, and then she was pulling me up, supporting me under the shoulder, and walking with me.

4

Physical contact had a way of making my powers stronger, even sometimes bringing some of the toucher into my mind. As an example, in this case Cheri wasn't the least bit scared, more excited. It was like we were on a roller coaster and she knew the amazing fall and loop-de-loops were coming. While some people would piss their pants at those loop-de-loops, it turned her on, made her want to scream and throw her hands up.

To my relief, that same emotion was passing into me at the moment. A bit of her craziness maybe, but hey, it was only temporary. Soon we were able to walk faster, then a slow jog, and I found I didn't need her help but was very curious as to why I'd received it.

"What's happening here?" I asked.

"Pretty sure your side's losing," she said. "A famous inmate, one they call Muerta, orchestrated it with some help. But a group of supers is chasing her down, and—"

"No, I mean you, here. Why're you helping me?"

She looked at me like I was the crazy one and laughed. "Because we're friends, silly goose pimple."

"I think it's just… never mind. Friends?"

"You wouldn't have helped me back there otherwise." She grinned, pulling on one of her pigtails and pointing to the smiley face on her tit. "You made me happy."

The visual wasn't necessary, but it wasn't bad to look at. I turned away, eyes going wide with the realization that I might have just absorbed another emotion from her—if you could call horniness an emotion. Apparently, my helping her hadn't simply made her happy, it had turned her on. Or something along the way had.

"Listen," I started, trying to think of an excuse to go our separate ways.

"Yeah?" she slowed, looking at me with confusion.

But as I thought about it, she'd proven herself valuable, kicking those two supers' butts back there. And so what if she was horny or making me feel the same way? I wasn't about to act on it. I was stronger than that. I was Ezra FUCKING Faldron, the law! Not some teenage boy prone to acting on his every whim.

My eyes drifted back over to the smiley face, though, and the cleavage above it. Certainly enough there that if I tore off her shirt and grabbed hold, I'd have more than a handful each.

"You feeling okay?" she asked, and I was about to ask why as my eyes rose from her breasts, but just then hit a tree. Damn, that hurt. I stumbled back, collected myself, and then cursed.

"Shit," I said, turning back toward where we'd come. "We need a plan."

"I thought you had a plan."

"Me?" I frowned, shaking my head. "I've been following you."

"Following me?" She laughed out loud. "Sugar-butt, following me will just get you in circles every time. Trust me, I'm me… so I know."

"Okay, can we just…" I gestured to the side of the hill, looking around for any sign of pursuers.

She shrugged and looked at the hill, kicked at the dirt to make a bit of a seat, and then sat. Interestingly, I noted how she kept her legs together like a lady.

"What is it?" she asked.

"You're here, with me... you're supposed to be in the asylum."

She beamed. "Isn't it funny how life works out sometimes?" Her finger started twirling her blue hair. "I mean, ever since you captured me I've gone back and forth on wanting to gut you or fuck you, and here we are."

Her smile continued as if she'd just explained everything.

"Have you... settled on one or the other of those?"

She laughed. "Of course I don't want to gut you."

The implication was, therefore, the alternative. Sometimes feeling emotions bothered me, like that very moment. She was clearly aroused by me again, and I couldn't say I wasn't feeling the same back at her. Putting my hands up to my mouth, I remembered my temple training, focused on blocking everything else out. Concentrate on the moment, let it happen,

"If we stay put, they might find us... then we're dead," I pointed out. Not scared by it, but noting the likely truth. "If we move, the chances are probably similar, but not if we get into hiding and figure out how we're going to beat this."

"What you're saying is, wait... that you want to get me in a dark, secluded place? Just the two of us?"

She adjusted her seat, and whether intentionally or not, the edge of her ass showed and just the hint of turquoise panties underneath the red mini-skirt. I swallowed, reminding myself that she was a nut job and a criminal, not someone to have those kinds of thoughts about.

"I'm not *not* saying that," I said, "but I don't think I'm saying it like you think I'm saying it."

She grinned and shrugged, her pigtails bouncing. "Whatever you say, boss."

"Just… come on." I motioned her up and started focusing on my survival training, scouting locations along the hillside and mountains that could be natural hiding spots for us to seek shelter. As dark as it was, without lights or anything to guide us, it wasn't easy.

We came to a small stream. She looked like she was about to drink from it, but I held out a hand. "It could have traces of acid. Look." I pointed in the direction it was coming from, toward the Chaos Zone.

"But I'm thirsty," she pouted.

"We'll find something, I promise." A look around made me less certain, only trees and barren lands. "Probably have to head back when the fighting dies down, look for supplies. Maybe there's something left on my ship."

"Didn't look like it," she replied. "Plus, others were already ransacking the remains."

"Fuck me."

She grinned, but I kept walking, not letting her comment on that.

"You must be used to this," she said, catching up. "All the hunting, no?"

"You're right. It's not the first time I've found myself stranded up shit creek, and won't be the last."

"Tell me the worst."

"The worst?" I racked my brain, crouching instinctively at the sound of another explosion. Would it ever end? "There's some competition, but maybe the time I was on Xandos, tracking down this real nasty piece of work named Suari—"

"He's so nice!" She grinned, then her face contorted into a frown. "Wait, you were hunting *him*?"

"Big belly, kinda reminds you of a rhino?"

"You mean the way his dick is like this huge rhino horn? Yeah, I always said that it's like—"

"The fuck?" I interrupted. "No, I—I didn't see that thanks be to Oram. Just, because he's huge and has that mole on his nose. You slept with that guy?"

She laughed. "Hell no, with that rhino horn he'd tear me in two! I'm petite, didn't you notice?"

"Ah…" My mind was racing with images of that, and it was not pleasant.

Her face took on an awkward, perplexed expression. "You were saying?"

"Right… So, on Xandos, *not* looking at his dick, and I was tracking him through this swamp, wading right up to my chest, when something brushes against my leg. At this point, I have nowhere to go, and I'll be honest, things brushing against me in water freaks me out. A couple more steps and I start realizing it's not just water—the swamp has a layer of blood to it, and is getting hot."

"No…"

"Right? What kind of swamp has blood and is hot, I wanted to know. Well, at the time I just wanted to be anywhere else but there, but I had to get my payday, right? Put that bastard behind bars." An uneasy feeling came over me, and I glanced over to see Cheri got really nervous at that statement. "Sorry."

"Keep going. I want to hear what the deal was."

"I mean, it's easy. Why I'm glad you weren't… you know, sleeping with the guy. It was his dumping ground for bodies, many not quite dead when he put them in there, and that was my first exposure to a hybrid."

She frowned and shook her head.

"Not familiar?" I asked.

"Enlighten me, dear educator," she replied with enough sarcasm to blow a house down.

"Right, most people don't know." I debated telling her but figured there was no harm at this point. "They've been popping up, mostly on the dark planets, beyond the fringe, you know. I thought it was only a rumor before that, but... then I saw her."

"Oh my god, what the fuck did you see already?" She turned and grabbed me, hysterical. "WHAT?"

I would've laughed if the memory wasn't bothering me so much. "I was, pushing through that yuck, and it brushed me again, then grabbed hold and pulled me under. I couldn't see a damn thing, at least... not until the light was almost on me."

"Light?"

"What are those fish called, the ones with a light hanging over them?" I knew the name, it just wasn't coming to me.

"You were scared of an *angler fish*?" She burst into laughter, but I covered her mouth, to keep from drawing attention. She was holding me, me with my hand on her mouth, and we stood there like that, totally aware of the awkwardness.

Finally, I released her and shifted out of her embrace—not sure where that came from—and said, "No. A super hybrid—part super, part angler fish.

Teeth covered in fresh blood, eyes yellow and crazed, and that fucking light, that horrible light coming right at me, inches away as I caught hold of her arms and tried to keep her off. She had claws too, and…" I shuddered at the thought, trying not to get lost in the moment.

"Damn. So like a vampire mermaid? Did she have the fish tail and all?"

I nodded. "Vampire mermaid… it's almost funny, if I hadn't seen the thing. See, your rhino friend was part of an illegal network of supers trafficking for experiments. That was just the first of them I came across."

"But… the story can't end there," she said as we started walking again. "What happened next? Did she bite you and turn you into a vampire? Oooh, do you want to suck my blood?"

"No, she didn't turn me into a vampire."

"Sure, I can see that. You were out in the daylight and all, but… what happened? Did you live?"

I turned to her, sure she was joking, but she really looked nervous for me. "Spoiler, I lived." Laughing at the relief on her face, I added, "Also, the vampire mermaid wasn't so hard to defeat… just terrifying. She wasn't very strong, see. Maybe new to this living in water thing, or maybe that was her power and she just hadn't gotten used to whatever hybrid procedure had made her that way. Either way, as long as I stayed away from her teeth I figured it was safe, so I managed to get around behind her and apply a chokehold. My breath nearly ran out before hers, but once I realized her gills needed to be covered, easy. Then I swam to the top to find rhino dick about to take a piss—okay, yeah, I did see it. That thing was disgustingly monstrous—"

"Right?"

"Anyway, I lunged, pinning his foot to the ground with a knife and narrowly avoiding his piss, and then was out of the water taking him down."

She looked at me, nodding excitedly, then stopped. "Wait, that's it? Sounds kinda easy."

"You try swimming in blood and have a vampire mermaid thing come after you, then almost get pissed on," I defended myself. "It was horrible."

"Worse than that time you were buried in the sand of Yinta, with those sand snakes all around you, eating at your flesh?"

I turned, impressed. "You've done your homework."

"Actually, I know a lot about you. Kind of a stalker. Want to know a secret?" She leaned in, mouth open in a wide smile, then whispered, "I let you catch me."

"Bullshit."

"It's true. Only way I could get to know you, I figured." She looked at me and crossed her eyes, sticking her tongue out, and then laughed. "Or maybe that's all bullshit, who knows!"

With that she ran ahead, her little red skirt flapping up and down to show her turquoise panties, her pigtails bobbing.

I had no idea what I was doing with her, but she was fun. After a glance around to ensure we were still in the clear, I followed. Soon we were deep in the forest, well enough away from the now-periodic fighting to have less to worry about. Still, others could've come out this way too, so I kept my wits about me.

When we sat to take a break, she alternated between staring at me and then lying back to gaze up at the stars. Then we got moving again, hoping to find something else back here, some form of shelter maybe or more guard houses I wasn't aware of, but so far, nothing. When we'd gone too far, we veered left to sort of circle back, as I worked out a better plan.

"How old were you?" she asked after a healthy amount of awkward silence.

"Excuse me?"

"First kill. How old?"

"I prefer not to kill, actually."

"But you killed the vampire fish."

"True." She had me there, and that certainly hadn't been the first time I'd had to take a life. But I don't know, for some reason this didn't feel like an area I wanted to let her into. All of this was too much, especially considering the situation. I'd already opened up to her a bit but had been starting to think that was a mistake. She was a villain and belonged in the asylum. Glancing over, I saw her scrunching her nose, looking at me with curiosity.

With a shrug, she started skipping, and I had to take longer strides to keep up.

"Wait, did you read my thoughts?" I asked between breaths, starting to feel the exertion already. "Or... the voices told you? I didn't mean it like that,"

"Look, I get it," she said, skipping along. "You think I'm crazy because I act crazy, but really I act crazy because I am crazy. See?"

"Not at all."

"I'm a complicated beast, like an onion but more delicious. If you ever want to peel me open and find out, maybe you'll understand. I don't know. I think it would hurt though."

While I wanted to ask her what the hell she was talking about, I figured doing so would only encourage her to keep on blabbing about this nonsense, so instead smiled politely and said, "I'll do that."

"Peel me open?" she gasped, and I sensed a hint of fear from her. "You wouldn't?"

"What?"

"Okay, let's just be clear." She stopped, grabbing me by the arm and spinning me around. "Are you talking about like, using a knife to open me up, or is this some metaphorical way of saying you want to sleep with me?"

To not stare at her in confusion was hard. I could tell she didn't like that, that it made her feel attacked, but following her logic and train of thought was bewildering.

"I don't have any intention of doing either," I said, slowly, and then pointed to the hillside. "There. That's where we'll regroup."

"Ah, regroup," she said with a wink.

I didn't even bother to comment, instead leading the way. It was a better location than I'd hoped for, complete with a spot that went into the hill in a half-cave, trees hanging over the entrance, and a freshwater source past it.

First thing I did was get a drink. I plopped down on the dirt, one hand running through my hair as I tried to consider our next move. Cheri sat across from me, cross-legged. Though her skirt somewhat covered her down there, it was still suggestive as hell. Even more so when she leaned forward and said, "Truth or dare."

"Unless the dare is 'I dare you to find us a way out of this mess,' I'm not interested."

She pouted, then said, "Truth for me. Cheri, why are you helping this asshole who tried to kill you and then sell you for a bounty? Answer, because he was just confused, he didn't know the real you yet, and wouldn't have done all that mean stuff if he had. That, and he's kinda cute."

"I'm not sure this is how it's played," I stated.

"Since you're not playing, I have to figure out how to play on my own, as I don't know the rules."

"You don't know the rules of Truth or Dare?"

She pouted and shook her head. "I wasn't exactly invited to the parties, you know. Not since the incident."

"Do I want to know what the incident was?"

"Not if you think little kids should be confined to bathrooms when wanting to relieve themselves. I'm not some prisoner who does my business where they tell me, I'm not—"

"I think I get the picture."

"Good," she said, grinning. "Speaking of which." Without another word, she glanced around, took a few steps away, and then pulled down her panties as she squatted to take a piss. "Cheri, I dare you to piss while this guy is watching."

"Oh, come on," I protested.

She ignored me as the tinkle started. At least I wasn't turned on anymore. And actually, that was a good thing, because my head was clearing and I was beginning to think about the direction of the asylum compared to where we were now, and what our options were.

If we could get to my ship and scavenge a few parts from the comms equipment, even if it didn't work, I was confident we could attach it to the equipment in the asylum and get in touch with a colleague or two. They wouldn't come out of duty or the goodness of their hearts, but I had some good credits to offer up as payment.

A new round of shooting started, a ship taking off and then a moment later being hit by something, only to careen back down and, judging by the sound of it, explode. Things were heating up back over at the Asylum.

"We have to lie low," I said, looking out at the darkness as bursts of light and more explosions went off. "It's too crazy out there."

"Crazy…?"

"Bad choice of words."

Cheri considered it, then shrugged. "Personally,

I've always liked the label, but I like psycho even better. Call me Miss Psychobitch, one hundred percent."

"I'm not calling you that."

"Why not?"

I shifted to see her, an orange glow lighting up her face and then fading. "It's offensive."

"Fuck that. Don't I get to decide what's offensive to me?" She scooted closer, leaning toward me in a way that I hadn't yet decided whether it was nice or made me uncomfortable. "Here's my point—I do what I want when I want. I don't live by their norms, what *they* tell me is the best way to behave, so they label me psycho? Fuck yeah! I say that word means freedom. And bitch because I won't cower before any man or woman. Because when I see bullshit, I call it out. Strength. Strength and freedom equal psychobitch, and I own it."

I smiled, shaking my head. Maybe it was the exhaustion, or maybe the pure honesty coming from her right then, but she seemed to be making a good point. "Fine, it's not horrible. But I'm not calling you a psychobitch. My mom taught me better than that."

"You can be one too, you know. Mr. Psychobitch, why not?" She grinned, this time putting a hand on my leg. "It's so crazy, right? Or psycho, to break gender norms of the word 'bitch,' that you're afraid to wear that label?"

I frowned, glanced at her hand, and shrugged. "No. I don't know. Maybe."

"Well, Mr. Psychobitch, let's do it—you and me and whoever else we find. We'll be psychobitches and tear this place up. Those fuckers want to stand in our way? I say we don't let them. Does this mean I forgive you for throwing me in that cell and being a real asshole? No, but... I'm willing to admit you're badass in a fight, know how to survive... and are probably a good lay."

My eyebrow arched at that. "I'm not going to sleep with you."

"Because it's against societal norms?" She scoffed, then added in a mocking voice, "Oh no, we just met and she was my prisoner and I don't know if I can get it up because she's a strong, powerful woman and rules say it's not proper."

"That's not exactly—"

"Fuck that!" she interrupted. "Be a Psychobitch."

Again, my eyes went to her hand on my leg, watched as it started to creep up my thigh. Her emotions were washing over me like a warm breeze —authentic, caring. Strange... but it was enough to make me go for it.

I leaned in and, eyes open the whole time in case

she surprised me with a knife to my throat or something, pressed my lips to hers. Her reaction caught me off guard, grabbing me by the shoulders and slamming me to the ground, then coming back in for a kiss so passionate it was like we were long-lost lovers finally reunited. Her lips were moist, her tongue teasing me, flicking across mine, and then she gently nibbled on my lower lip.

When she pulled back, I saw she was straddling me, chest heaving as her eyes took me in. She went for her top, playing with the shoulder of it, eyeing me as if asking if I was ready. And then she laughed.

"Holy shit, you were really going to do it, huh?" she asked.

"Wait, what?"

"Go all the way, right here when we could be killed at any minute. Fuck, you're crazier than I am!" She leaned in, kissed me again, and whispered into my ear as her hand moved down toward my crotch, "That's hot."

Her hand went to my thigh, creeping down between my legs, and then she pinched my thigh and laughed.

I stared at her for a minute, then said, "I'm pretty sure you're mean."

Her grin widened at that. "Oh, you don't like a tease? Trust me, I'm not one at all. You'll see—I'm going to fuck you so hard you'll shrivel up from all the cum leaving you. But not here, not like this. Shit, I may be batso, but we need to live through this and," she lowered her voice, gesturing over her shoulder with her thumb, "there are three of those bastards sneaking up on us."

"What?" I pushed out from underneath her, cringing as my boner nearly bent with the quick movement. Readjusting myself, I cursed at my carelessness and took up a defensive position. "How do you know?"

"Part of my powers," she said, cuddling up behind me and running her hand along the inside of my thigh again. "It's what drove me a bit insane to begin with, the docs say. Voices, thoughts… I can't hear them, but they're there. They sort of mumble, but I can get a sense of what they're going on about. Like yours, for instance—you wanted to fuck me soooo bad."

"Can you… not?" I said, moving her hand. "I'm trying to focus." Her hand was on my pistol next, pulling it free. "And…"

I stopped, as she had moved back, aiming it at me.

"Why the fuck do I have powers suddenly?" she asked.

Here I was at an impasse. I couldn't exactly tell

her about the Quencher I kept on me, or how it let me use my powers in spite of stopping others a certain distance away... to some degree. It wasn't perfect.

"There's nobody, is there?" I asked.

"Answer me, first."

I decided to bend the truth a bit, for now. "It's how my powers work. The SupraTech Quencher doesn't work on me... because I'm an amplifier. If you're close, same effect." There were amplifiers out there, and it was possible this could be true about how they worked in these circumstances. It was hard to say, and she wasn't likely to be able to prove it one way or another.

She considered me for a moment, then grinned. "Three of 'em, like I said. But right now I'm debating who I have the better chances with, them or you."

"Is that so?" This was an unfortunate change of events, but at least my boner was gone.

"On the one hand, what I said is true." She pouted, eyes moving across me. "And I really do want to fuck you—in a sexual way, not like leave you stranded or shoot you kind of fuck you, like fuck you over—"

"I got it."

"Right. So on the one hand, betraying you feels wrong. On the other, there's more of them."

My eyes didn't leave hers as I contemplated my next move, wondering how in the hell I could've missed this. My empath abilities should've been able to sense her change in emotions. But no, actually, if she was as crazy as I'd originally thought, this made sense. Maybe her mind hadn't changed at all? She'd simply acted, or there was more than one mind in there? It was all too confusing, but I decided to take the gamble.

"We take them out, together. You and me… the Psychobitches." Noting the way the pistol lowered and her lip turned up, I kept going. "Once we're in the clear, we find a good spot, and maybe it's me who fucks your brains out. Make this team official with a good ol' skin bonding."

I was one hundred percent talking out of my ass, but the simple fact was that this crazy lady was pointing a gun at me and, for some reason, wanted me. As much as I'd always made a rule *not* to fool around with my prey, I found myself in a very awkward predicament and could argue that the situation had changed enough to where maybe I'd do it. I wasn't committed in my mind yet, but all the anxiety over our situation was piling up and needed a means of release.

And then there was the way she'd opened up to me—very confusing when put with this whole betrayal thing, but I could overlook it, maybe, if she'd just hand over the pistol.

"Here's the deal," she finally said, and lowered the pistol but held out her other hand to motion for me to stay back. "I gotta know I can trust you. That we're really a team… right? You want to know you can trust me, too?"

"Yeah," I replied, cautiously.

"Good. So it's settled then. I hold onto the pistol and shoot those fuckers, you do your punchy-kick thing if I miss, and then we fuck like rabbits. I look forward to the plowing, good sir."

What the fuck.

That's all my mind could come up with, so when she stuck out her hand for me to shake, instead of taking her down or taking action like the cop side of me said to do, I simply took her hand and shook.

"I'm glad we have an accord," she said with a wink and then abruptly turned, heading toward the direction of our supposed trespassers.

Hey, at least she wasn't shooting me. Yet.

5

Moving out under the trees, the first thing I noticed was a dark blur of movement to my right. Out of range for my empath abilities, which were generally activated by proximity, and heightened by touch.

I motioned in that direction, but Cheri shook her head, causing her pigtails to wave back and forth like a Chinese drum toy, and then she motioned straight ahead. I knew what I saw, but she pointed again, and then whispered, "You're tracking the prey. I want the hunters."

Using terms that were often related to my profession, but that were now switched around like this didn't sit well with me, but I had to agree. In this insanity, any group that was hunting down lone wolves was likely to be of the bully variety, and often no good.

"Fine," I hissed and followed Cheri.

We were back in the woods, the sound of fighting still going on in the distance, but here it was still, almost quiet. At least, it was until a flash appeared in the sky, apparently getting everyone's momentary attention because the sounds of gunfire stopped.

"All rebels, all inhabitants of Abaddon Asylum, and all others who are not where you belong," a voice rang out in the night. "Orion Corp sees this as a direct attack and has therefore deemed all further action an act of war. We realize, however, that some of you are our soldiers and will stand for the side of right. Therefore, here is the deal we offer—as enemies have been shooting down our drones, all we can offer is high level feeds for those back home, but this is a special edition of Abaddon for them tonight. It's not just the Chaos Zone anymore!"

I shared a look with Cheri, both of us knowing this wasn't good. Essentially, the corporation was turning the asylum portion of the planet into a kill zone. And the message wasn't done.

"For those of you wishing to say 'fuck you' to Orion Corp., well here's a big fuck you back. For those of you loyal or wishing to join the Orion Corp., we have an opportunity! If you want to escape this place before we wreak havoc and kill off most of you, enslaving the rest, guess what?" The voice got excited here as if it were some guy very into the idea of all this, which disturbed me—this was Orion Corp.! My employer, the organization so many of my peers worshiped. It just... didn't fit. As he continued, the voice got higher and higher, saying, "You all get to kill the idiots and weaklings for us! Team up, form a posse or gang or whatever you want to call it and end the rest of these rebels—those who are to blame, who started this mess. Find them and bring us their heads, and we'll see that you get off this planet alive. You'll be the lucky few! And guess what, A.I. and advanced world-scanning system, we can monitor it all so that you too will have the chance to join our army!

"The fuck?" I said, turning to see that Cheri was sitting down cleaning her nails, seemingly not paying any attention.

"That's right," the voice continued. "You get enough kills in the next twenty-four hours and form the team that takes down the rebels, you will be able to leave from these coordinates. The clock has started, and remember—if they aren't dead nobody leaves!"

Fireworks burst out into the sky as if this was all some big celebration, and I plopped down next to

Cheri, watching the display as I tried to wrap my head around this.

"Why would Orion Corp. throw us all into the vat like this?" I asked. "It doesn't compute."

Cheri scoffed, then leaned her head on my shoulder and looked up at me as if we were an adoring couple. "You're so cute when you're stupid."

"What are you talking about?" I gently nudged her head away.

"You're serious?" she asked, looking at me, then laughing. "Oh my… you are!" She pushed herself up, shaking her head, hands out like she couldn't believe what was going on. "Here I was thinking you were awesome but kinda evil, kinda going after the money like a jerk, but no… you're just stupid."

"Now would be a good time to stop insulting me and explain."

"Dickface," she said, turning on me and sticking her fingertip on my nose. "Has there ever been a moment where I haven't said Orion Corp. is evil?"

"Did you?" I asked, seriously not remembering.

"Me and mine have done bad things, sure, but mostly against Orion Corp. and never as bad as what they've done to our world. You want to take down the bad guys? That's where you start. Orion Corp. fucking headquarters. Got it?"

I blinked, and for once her emotions were simply

pure, no craziness going on, no weird ulterior motives... just passion and true belief in what she was saying.

But I couldn't accept that. It threw everything I'd been living for on its head. I stood, turning back to face the end of the fireworks, my world potentially shattered. Odd, how something like that can make you totally forget about three people hunting others in the woods. That little fact nearly got me killed if Cheri hadn't lunged for me, connecting with my thigh and taking me to the ground as a large man came charging, his rusty, serrated blade slicing the air just above my head.

I spun, back in the game, and watched as the other two came for us. What made this worse, was now I wasn't sure where all of these people fell on the scale of good to bad. Had I been the bad one all these years? Were they now trying to kill us because they saw Cheri and me as the ones Orion Corp. had just called for to be killed?

One of them had her by the left pigtail, yanking her around and lifting what looked like a hubcap above his head to bring down on her. At that moment I was certain of one thing—she'd been honest with me, at least to the amount that she knew how, and there was no way in hell I was going to let this fucker hurt her.

My stun baton hit him first, sending him into shock at the same time as Cheri's foot had apparently connected with his nuts. The result was that she took a portion of the shock, and when he went flying back, she curled up in a ball of pain. Fuck, that hadn't gone as planned. The other guy was still incoming though, and the third had turned to rejoin the party.

The serrated blade caught my attention, but not as much as the guard-issued shotgun the second guy had just turned to level on me. As much as I hated taking lives, the minute someone aimed a gun at me, they were dead.

So it was that I didn't even think, my hand drawing my backup pistol and firing. A hole appeared in the fucker's throat, another in his forehead, and then my pistol was back in its holster as I spun to take on the guy with the blade.

"Careful next time, asshole," Cheri said, finally pushing herself to her feet and running to take on Hubcap, while I twirled my baton and squared off against this guy.

His eyes roamed over me, focused on the words police. He froze, sniffed, and said, "I smell bacon. That mean you're with Orion Corp.?"

"Could be," I said.

"Well, shit man, we're on your side. We—"

THWUNK!

The hubcap hit him in the face, Cheri charging in after it to snatch it up as both it and the man fell, and then she was on him, slamming it into his face repeatedly until there wasn't much face left.

At least I'd known he was on the side of Orion Corp., though I was still very confused about whether that meant he was on the side of good or evil. If he was on the planet, he was most likely bad in some way, regardless, so I swallowed down any sense of moral quandary I might have on the topic, and said, "Nice work."

Cheri stood and then strolled back up to me, looking all kinds of pissed. Her hand shot out and slapped me in the nuts, not hard, but enough to make my stomach clench up and for my legs to want to give out.

"Next time, try saving me in a way that doesn't make me almost piss myself."

"Deal," I said through gritted teeth.

"Good." She glared a minute longer, then bent over, smiling as she talked to my crotch. "Sorry about that, boys, I promise to make it up to you later."

"Now that that's over…" I said, the pain subsiding. "Hello?" We both turned, looking for any sign of their prey. "We're not going to hurt you."

"He's a really nice guy," Cheri chimed in, giving me a wink. "Hot, too. Check out his ass."

There was a long silence, followed by a series of lines suddenly appearing in the sky and moving down at us. For a second I thought they might be some form of crazy lasers and we'd be cut to shreds, but when they met the ground and vanished, replaced with a yellow humanistic form of the same light, I knew what this was—Orion.

"Cheri, Tier Four Criminal," the voice from earlier said, the being of light facing her. When it turned to me, it hesitated. "Ezra Faldron, Tier Four Orion Ally. Bounty Hunter... But you shouldn't be here."

"My ship was caught in the uprising," I said. "If you have an option for getting me out, I'm all ears."

The being tilted its head, then said, "Like the rest. Although..." It hesitated, then stepped closer, voice lowered. "We might have a special ship at the same time—that one as a distraction. It's meant for guards, but you might qualify. See that the leader of this uprising is taken down, and you have a ticket home."

"Great. My years of service don't earn me that?"

The being of light stared at me then turned, looking around, scanning. Finally, it said, "Erupa, Tier Three. Criminal. Good luck to each of you, all are registered in the system. Should you prove useful, loot crates will be dropped. We have to make it fun to watch, after all."

With that, the light turned back into lines and rose out of there, leaving us in relative darkness.

"Um," Cheri finally spoke up, "it's not like we didn't hear it, Erupa. You coming out, or what?"

"Well bend me over and call me silly," Erupa said, stepping out of the shadows as if none of that just happened. It looked like we might have another member of our team—if she didn't try to skewer me with her horns, that is.

6

"Here I was thinking they would've killed you off by now," Erupa said, looking us over. "And I see you've already captured this crazy bitch again."

"Psychobitch," Cheri corrected her.

Erupa frowned, then growled, taking an offensive stance. "I ain't going down without a fight."

"On him or me?" Cheri asked. "Or neither? Just want to make sure we're all clear."

If her strategy was to confuse and annoy Erupa, it was working. Before the demon lady lost it and charged, though, I figured I'd better step in.

"She's not my prisoner," I said. "After what happened back there, we're just trying to survive."

"That so?" Erupa glanced over at Cheri. "And the... er, Psychobitch, here?"

"We need each other, as you need us. If you want to get out of this mess alive."

"Or I join those fuckheads." Erupa motioned to one of the dead men nearby. "Apparently, they're building up a little gang. You don't think they'd want me?"

"I don't think anyone should offer themselves up to a group of mentally deranged criminals," I countered. "But at the moment, some might say we fall into that category. Dammit, I don't know... I've no idea what's going on back there, but you can be sure it won't be pleasant. No tea and fucking crumpets, if you get my drift."

She glared, and I knew I had her attention. It was us or be out on her own. She could use our help, and we hers.

"I'm not forgetting how I got here," she said, glaring at me. "Nor will I sleep with my back to you. But you're right, at least you're predictable. Them? I can't say the same of them."

"Thanks for the reminder," I said, glancing between her and Cheri.

"You can trust us," Cheri said with a shrug. "Because if we wanted to kill you, you'd be dead already."

"I kinda want to kill him," Erupa admitted. "But it's not in my best interest... yet."

"See," Cheri said with her silly grin. "What I meant was, if it were advantageous for us to kill you, you'd be dead already."

"Please let me know slightly before I become not advantageous, if you could," I said.

"Deal," Erupa replied. "If you agree not to sell us out again—we get to a point where you choose between splitting paths and selling us out, you go your separate way. Got it?"

"Of course."

"On your honor?"

"On my life, my honor..." I noticed Cheri flicking her tongue across her teeth, shaking her head. "What?"

"Not enough," Cheri said. "What do those things mean to a man? Swear on your tiggle and bits."

"My...?"

"Cock and balls," she said, rolling her eyes as if that wasn't enough. "You swear by those, that's legit."

"I thought we were already on the same side," I pointed out.

"Still, now that Erupa brings it up, I'm with her. I want to hear it."

I turned to Erupa in frustration, as if she'd take my side. Naturally, she didn't. She stood there, hands on hips, waiting.

"I swear on my cock and balls." The words

sounded weird, so I was surprised when Cheri acted like a grown-up for once and didn't joke or giggle, but nodded, then turned to Erupa to see if that was good enough for her.

"That is, assuming he has a cock and balls," Erupa said, giving me a devilish grin, the image being aided by the horns on her head.

"Oh, he does. I nut-checked him not long ago, even felt them give, you know the way you can tell if you've made contact, by how it's kinda squishy and—"

"Enough," Erupa said, eyes wide. She actually turned to me and said, "Does she ever turn off?"

"No," I replied. "But we need to get moving. After that little message, they'll be after more blood."

"I saw a place, that way," Erupa said. "When I was running, but I figured I'd lead those bastards away from it and double back."

"Like, lodging?"

She nodded.

"Great, I could kill for a good long nap," Cheri said. Neither of us had the heart to tell her that wouldn't likely be possible, not with only twenty-four hours to figure out how to escape this place.

It was starting to get cold, so we walked faster, eyes searching our surroundings for any sort of shelter.

"It was just this way," Erupa promised, taking us down a small ridge, and then pausing to search. She seemed to recognize something, and she kept us moving in that direction. "So, I imagine the plan is to take out the leader of the uprising?"

"Someone will," I replied. "Not our job."

"But that's your ticket out of here," Cheri said. "Ours too, if we wanted to play hitmen for Orion. I won't, so that leaves you."

"Maybe," I agreed. "But that's what *they* tell me my ticket is. I'm wondering if there's another way."

Both looked at me with surprise, but it was Erupa who spoke up. "Mr. Law, thinking outside the box? You surprise me."

"Maybe I don't know if I can trust them anymore," I replied. "Maybe I shouldn't have been living by their rules for so long. Or maybe I'll get out of here and it'll all make sense—I don't know. But right now I'm not making rash decisions, nor am I jumping to conclusions."

"Good for you, sugar-butt," Cheri said, and then pointed. "Oooh, ooh, there!"

Sure enough, hidden between some trees and not easily visible because it was built into the hill, there was a door along with a metal wall. It looked suspicious to me, but honestly, I had no idea what the people of this planet were up to out here on a routine basis. Even if they were killing people or doing whatever else, it couldn't be as bad as what was going on in the asylum area at the moment.

We found the door locked, and cursed, looking for something to break it. Erupa swore again, saying that if she had her powers, she'd be able to get it open. I tried ignoring the look from Cheri, but finally scooted close to Erupa and said, "Give it a try, you never know."

She frowned, but mumbled, "What the hell. Why not?" and stepped up to the door. Prying her nails inside, she got her fingers partially around the door and gave a mighty heave.

"It actually worked!" she said, looking down at her arms and marveling. With a glance back to us, she said, "Maybe the Quencher's on the fritz?"

"Yeah, maybe," I said and followed her in.

The place had three small rooms, the back, too, separated by a hallway. All of the walls and even the floor were metal, giving the impression of a large air duct. No lights, only the dim glow from slits along the top that acted like windows, though it would've been quite annoying when rain came, if ever. I'd often wondered about the weather on Abaddon, knowing it was controlled on the Chaos Zone side, so why not over here? They had other ways to keep the trees watered, surely.

We made our way to the back of the second room, exhaustion taking over, and I mumbled about wanting to sit for a minute, to maybe rest my eyes. Shooting in the distance became like a rhythmic lullaby. They continued to explore, and when I opened my eyes again, Cheri was squatting close enough to reach and touch me, staring.

"What?" I asked, my empath powers getting some seriously interesting patterns from her.

"What we'd said. You know, 'Take care of them, get somewhere private and...'" She didn't even bother to say the rest but started undoing the red, semi-concealing body armor top. It fell to the floor with a clank, leaving her breasts fully exposed. I almost expected to see that same yellow smiley face on her left tit, but no, just two, perfectly shaped perky breasts. Her nipples were darker than I'd expected, making me wonder if her hair was naturally dark—I often found a correlation there. It wasn't until she moved that the light caught on metal and I realized the left nipple was pierced. Sexy, in a strange way, but also made me think of pain.

"Wow," was all I could think to say. It had been too long since I'd been with a woman, and the sight of breasts in an intimate way was really pulling at my libido, which was in turn pleading with me to act.

She grinned at me. "Your turn."

"We're... really doing this?" I glanced around to ensure we were alone, torn between hoping we were and weren't. "Where's Erupa?"

"You want her involved?" she asked.

"No, that's not what I meant."

"Maybe next time. This time, I told her she was on first watch."

I gulped. Hey, I was part of the team now, wasn't I? One of these Psychobitches, maybe with Erupa now as part of the team, too.

Still not totally sure I was making the right move, I undid my protective vest, then my overshirt. Finally, I pulled off the white undershirt and stood there, watching her eyeing my muscular frame with anticipation.

She was about to slide her mini-skirt off when I held up a hand and started toward her. As much as I liked this idea of watching each other strip, I was the fucking law enforcement officer here. She wasn't going to dictate how this was to happen, not to me. So I stepped up, took her by the waist, and pulled her to me. First my lips met hers, then I kissed her neckline, hands moving along her side, up to cup her breast as my lips kissed down further, finding her nipple and massaging it with my lips and tongue. The metal surprised me, as I had forgotten about her piercing, and when she moaned, I felt her pleasure flowing through me as well. One of the interesting side effects of my power was feeling what my partner felt in these circumstances. It could be great, trust me! And, if they weren't into it, no amount of faking could convince me otherwise. In these circumstances, my power could be a curse or a blessing, but right now it was definitely the latter.

Her fingers were working violently at my belt. As I moved back up to kiss her neck, hands massaging her breasts and then moving down to her lower back, she got my pants undone.

A slightly cold hand slipped in, no playing around or hesitating as she grabbed my cock with firm intensity. My hands slipped into her miniskirt, grabbing handfuls of ass, and I squeezed as her hand stroked me, exploring me. More pleasure, now from her touch but also as she enjoyed the strength of my squeeze.

I slid off her skirt and panties, going with them so that I could kiss her pelvis, her inner thigh. She grabbed me by the hair and pulled me up, kissing me again, but wagging her finger. "Not yet."

At first, I thought she was about to tease me again and back out of this, but then she was slipping my pants off, both hands massaging my balls and then cock. She leaned against the wall, pulled me close, and then slid my cock inside of her. One leg wrapped around the back of my thigh and she was pulling me, thrusting, not letting me take charge no matter how much I tried. Finally, I just let it happen, doing it however she wanted, until after a few minutes of sweaty passion I realized she was biting her lip and yelping, eyes closed like she was in pain and I was fucking her harder than I'd ever fucked before.

I started to slow to ask her if she was okay, but she smacked me and grabbed my ass hard, fingernails digging into flesh, and growled, "Don't you dare fucking stop."

So I didn't. A few more thrusts and she was leaning back as if about to fall, eyes open and staring at me, emotions going crazy and tingling passing over to me so that I could feel her orgasm. Her eyes rolled back, closed again, and then she was leaning into me, holding me tight. The sensation of experiencing her orgasm made me start to orgasm too so that all it took was the clenching of her pussy to cause me to finally cum.

We stood there for a moment, enjoying it, unable to move from the intensity we'd just shared, and then finally she looked at me, all crazy gone, and gave me a gentle smile.

"You're wild."

I grinned, kissed her, and said, "That was... amazing."

She nodded, bit her lip and shrugged. "Team Psychobitches can't be broken apart now. We're formed as one."

My laugh was involuntary, but then I felt a sharp pain of hurt coming from her, so I quickly replaced my smile with a look of being dead serious as I repeated her words, "As one."

Her smile returned, and she lowered her leg, letting me fall out of her, and then we held each other another moment. I wasn't sure what she'd meant—like did she think we were married or something? Shit, it wasn't long ago she was my prisoner and I was handing her over for credits.

It was my fault, breaking my own rule by getting involved with one of the targets. In my defense, the whole uprising thing had changed it all, but now I was wondering what my inability to keep my dick in my pants had committed me to.

I let my power free, sensing what she was feeling right now, and suddenly didn't feel nervous or scared at all. Simply comforted, ready for whatever would come next. At times it was dangerous to do this because I might be overcome with rage or other emotions when there was no reason for me to be other than that I'd opened up the gates to the other person's emotions, but in this case, it proved to be the right move.

She took my hand in hers and grinned, her other hand taking one of her pigtails and twirling her hair around her pointer finger as her wide grin returned. "So, boss, you want to try to get Erupa in on this now, or…?"

"Quit it," I said, shaking my head. "Right now, all I want is to get you dressed so you don't freeze to death."

"It's not that cold," she pointed out, but pressed her nude body to mine, moving back and forth with her hips playfully. "I won't say no to this kind of warmth. But since we don't want the enemy to find us like this and have the advantage," she sighed and turned, bending over in a very sexual way to pick up her clothes, "I guess you're right."

Looking at that image of her bent over, her perfect ass and tight pussy showing the more she bent, was like looking at the sun and having sunspots in your vision for a few minutes after. Even as I started dressing, the image wouldn't leave my mind. I could almost reach out and touch it, even stick out my tongue and taste it. Hot damn, I was in for a crazy adventure.

And I meant that in every sense of the phrase.

7

A harsh kick to my side woke me to the image of a face with horns up close and personal. *Fuck, I was in Hell,* I thought, only to see that it was Erupa. Not bad to look at, once I realized she wasn't the devil here for my soul. Then again, I was on the planet Abaddon—there probably weren't many places closer to Hell than this.

"I found something," she said, nudging Cheri much more gently than the wake-up call she'd given me. Motioning for us to follow, she made for the back room.

We both trailed after her, sharing timid smiles and shy glances, until Erupa finally said, "You two can cut that shit out. I know you fucked—nothing to be ashamed of."

"I…" There wasn't anything to say to that, other than, "How?"

"You thought I was going to stay on watch forever? At one point I came back and saw you two, and honestly, it was hot so I watched you instead."

"You… watched us?" My mind was reeling with the thought of that, wondering what angle she'd seen me from as if that mattered, and why my mind hadn't picked up on her being nearby. Then again, it had been quite occupied.

"For next time, I've got pointers," she said and then laughed. "But don't worry, we might not live to see the next time."

"We don't need pointers," I said.

She chuckled, running a hand through her hair and then along one of her horns, mind elsewhere. "Trust me, you do."

As she entered the next room, Cheri caressed my arm and said, "Hey, you were amazing. Don't let her get into your head."

"Yeah?"

"Made me cum, didn't you?"

I was starting to feel good about that, when Erupa turned back and said, "Ah, but you could've made her cum, like, three or four times that I noticed, and same for you, Psychobitch Queen Bee."

"Cheri will do," Cheri replied. "Psychobitch Cheri

if you want to be formal. And hold the fuck up, me? I know how to work a cock, okay?"

"If you say so, but he could've multi-orgasmed."

"Guys don't have multiple orgasms, do they?" Cheri turned to me. "That's not a thing, right?"

"It is when they're with me," Erupa replied, then clapped her hands and said, "Hurry up, now. Stop getting distracted."

Cheri looked like she was bursting to find out what Erupa was going on about, and so was I, but when she took us to a side room—one hidden behind a cloth in the darkness, so that we hadn't seen it, we all froze at the sight in the middle of the room. A hole led into the ground, with crudely cut stairs leading into it, and then a tunnel that went in two directions.

"That's… interesting," I said, kneeling to try and have a look without going in. All I saw was darkness.

"Interesting, and possibly our way to do this," Erupa said.

"Are we still talking about the multiple orgasms or—" Cheri started.

"No, we're not. This could be the key to getting off this planet, not the key to getting off. This way here," she pointed left, "seems to lead back toward the asylum. The other way, who knows?"

"It's at least worth checking out," I admitted.

"Better than the whole lot of nothing we have to go off of otherwise."

"And then we get off?" Cheri asked. "Off-planet, I mean."

"If we get in there and take out as many of the rebels as we can, along with their leader, we have a chance, yes."

"Dark tunnels, my favorite," Cheri said with a frown, then she sneezed. "Agh, see? I'm allergic to them."

"You can't be allergic to dark tunnels," Erupa argued. "The dust, maybe."

"Tell that to my allergy," Cheri said, and then pursed her lips. "You two will have to go in there without me, get it done, and then come back and we go another way."

"Leaving you having not accomplished a damn thing," Erupa said, "which means not taking you off this planet."

"Well, cock-sucking lily pads." Cheri folded her arms, chin in her hand, and seemed to consider it. "Fine, I'm in."

"Of course you are," Erupa replied and then led the way down.

It was dark, but I didn't wear all of this cool police gear just to look cool, though it certainly helped. I'd come with glow sticks, a mini-flashlight, and more weapons if needed. At the moment, I turned on the flashlight, keeping a hand over it to give us light but not warn people down the tunnels we were coming. Hopefully there was no one around down there, but it's always good to play it safe.

"What made you do it, anyway?" Erupa said, after walking a bit. "Turn on your own, I mean?"

"Ooh, touchy subject." Cheri held a finger to her mouth, but I waved the comment away.

"I'm still not sure about all of this, honestly," I admitted.

"But you see what's going on," she countered. "Meaning you're either blind and don't see it, incredibly stupid because you see but don't understand, or… evil."

"I've been told my whole adult life you all are the ones to watch out for," I explained, hushing my voice in hopes that it would remind them where we were, and that we needed to keep a low profile. "It's not like I didn't know about Abaddon and Orion's involvement, all hunters who're anything know that. And there was an uprising, right? What are they supposed to do about that?"

"Um, not promise rewards for slaughtering those not involved, for one." She looked at Cheri for backup, but the blue-haired lady just smiled and nodded as if we were discussing ice cream flavors.

"It's barbaric, and not the worst of what they've done, you can count on that."

"You don't know what you're talking about."

"Oh?" She turned on me, voice growing much louder than was safe here. "How about the slaughter of Brendol?"

"Putting down anarchist rioters," I countered.

"The War of Derown?"

"To bring peace to all supers by setting an example that—"

"Fuck, don't say it. You've really drunk the piss, haven't you?"

"I can assure you that I've never imbibed any form of piss, real or metaphorical."

"To be fair to him," Cheri said. "He's learning. When this all started, he seemed really shaken. I think it's just a matter of time."

"Thank you," I said.

"He's like a small child we have to teach, though not that small," she reached over and pinched the tip of my dick, which I did not find appropriate or enjoy, given the timing.

"We're getting off track," I said, taking her hand and holding it in front of me so that she wouldn't do that again. "There's a way to get off this planet, and we have as good a chance as any. Better, actually. How about we focus on that, then look for the answers you both seem to think you have? I find out for myself. Deal?"

"He's more open-minded than most Orion hunters," Erupa admitted. "Deal."

"And for the record, the war of Derown was basically about who gets to have pets in their houses," Cheri said. "My friend survived the war and told me all about it."

Erupa and I turned on her, incredulous. Was that even worth addressing? We shared a look and shook our heads before continuing down the tunnel.

"Her name was Lilly," Cheri kept on, eyeing the ceiling as she spoke. "Her wings were bright green. The cutest bird ever, but one day she flew away, so I can only assume she decided it was time to return to her home planet."

It actually hurt my brain, thinking about how much was wrong with what she'd just said, but I continued walking, eyes scanning the darkness for any sort of sign that we weren't wasting our time down here.

We paused as light spilled into the tunnel ahead, then pulled back, crouching and pressing against the wall, the three of us closer than maybe Erupa would've liked. Ahead, we saw a group. They came right out of the wall, then moved down the hall, stopped at another section before glancing around, and then re-entering through there.

Once they were gone, we moved up to find no evidence of doors.

"Why's everything here so secretive?" Cheri asked.

"I'm guessing this was a place to smuggle people out from the asylum," I replied. "Not sure where or why, but if it leads from there to that house, and then to wherever those people were going, that's all that makes sense to me."

"Maybe an escape route?" Erupa posited. "I mean, it's possible some guards saw what was going on here and decided it wasn't right, so they started this system to help the inmates they didn't believe to be in the wrong."

It made as much sense as anything I could come up with, and much more than Cheri's idea when she started hypothesizing that maybe it was just for guards to take sex breaks.

"Out of curiosity," Erupa asked her. "Does your mind never leave the idea of sex, or is it your mouth that's to blame?"

"My mouth could definitely use more sex," she said with a grin, poking her tongue into her cheek so that it looked like she was sucking a dick—oddly, it was the part with her heart tattoo that was pushed out when she did it.

"Did you—" I started.

"Please don't ask," Erupa interrupted.

"For your information, I think of other stuff, but being in situations like this gets me all hot and bothered. It's exciting, the near death, the lack of knowing what might happen next. Tell me, Erupa, that the idea of riding his face doesn't sound great right now, especially with the sense of danger."

"I…" Erupa finally looked embarrassed, and I had to chuckle.

"First we'd probably have to not hate each other," I pointed out. "Use that as your starting defense."

"Right." She looked away, started down the hall, and then doubled back to the panel. "Maybe we should see where this goes."

We agreed, so worked it open and made our way in. The first room was simply a long metal corridor, not so different from the dark tunnel.

In here we were careful to keep quiet, listening for any sign that others might come walking through. Cheri gripped my arm, earning her a condescending glance from Erupa. All I could think was that this was incredibly stupid. If Orion Corp. soldiers came through at that moment, there was nowhere to go.

The hallway brought us to a glass elevator, but we didn't need to take it to see where it led. Down here, it wasn't just a planet that had been carved out. On the contrary, from the metal and glass and levels upon levels that continued down, I was quite certain we'd just discovered that Abaddon was a built-up space station. Not all rooms down there were visible, many cut off by metal walls and more tunnels, but it was enough to know that this problem was considerably larger than we thought it was.

Also, judging by the lines of robotic soldiers down below and to our left, it was quite clear Orion Corp. wouldn't have much of a problem taking out the rebels above. This bothered me even more, because if they had that kind of power lying around, why let the rebels overthrow the guards? Why even let it get this far?

Of course, the answer was quite simple, and now knowing their true nature, it came to me immediately—television ratings and money. It was all about the credits, those sick fucks.

As we were watching, a line of workers passed below, about to enter a doorway when lines of screens turned on. They all paused, turning to the screens, a couple of them cheering. Cheri was watching with anticipation radiating off of her, Erupa with unease.

"It's that time of day, ladies and gentlemen," a voice said as the screen flashed with a logo that said to place their bets, and sure enough the people we could see were pulling up devices and fidgeting with them, likely placing their bets on whatever was about to happen.

Next, the screens flashed to a long corridor of metal, with a wall of glass where an audience of several very wealthy men and women sat watching. When they saw they were on the screen, some nodded politely, others turned to avoid the camera.

The view switched to the empty tunnel, and the voice continued, "For your viewing pleasure, today we bring you two of the corporation's greatest soldiers—all yours, an army of one variety or both, for prices that will be discussed after your visit."

Since I was expecting soldiers, the sight of beasts entering from opposite ends of the tunnel surprised me. But then they reared up and it was clear these weren't beasts at all, but humans. Maybe supers with their animal characteristics? Some I'd known had cat or fox ears and tails, and there was Erupa with her horns. But this, this was different.

One of them had long hair hanging from all over its body, long claws extending out of his hands, and as we watched he sort of transformed into a nude, male form, then back, what could be best described as a bear shifter! The other, which I'd at first thought to be some sort of alien—the first I would've known about—turned to the camera and snapped its jaws, and now I understand what it was. Another man, this one had been transforming as he walked, and he now had the fully formed head of a shark! Fucking weird, and very disturbing. His body took on that shark-skin look, though it seemed to glimmer like metal, and his muscles grew larger as we watched, finally stopping at an impossibly huge size that I'd only seen before on a very few supers.

"One a natural land beast, the other notorious in Earth's oceans," the voice started up again, "this new breed of soldier can appear normal when needed, but when it comes to battle, you have what you see here. Or, if you're in the market for entertainment…" The voice and screen cut out, interrupted by a display of a woman in a skimpy outfit stepping into the room, flashing out for a second to show she was only a hologram.

She moved her body seductively, and then said, "Are you ready for a show?" Fake applause and cheers followed, and then she held up one fist and shouted, "Let's get it on!"

Electric pulses went through the room, shocking

the two shifters. Each let out snarls and roars, and then they were charging each other.

Blood sprayed, the room shook, and more of those damn fake cheers followed.

I wasn't about to watch another second of that. Now that we'd seen it, I registered what we were looking at. Many of the rooms where it appeared people were standing were holding cells. Squinting to get a better look, I could make out one of the people had a tail, another had what could be either long swords in his hands or long blades instead of hands.

I needed to see more. Fighting the pounding in my head that told me to turn back, I went to the ledge and looked down. There were many of these holding cells, too many to count. As if... holy shit, that was it! They were arrayed here for viewing from the glass elevator, as a demonstration for visitors. This was a fucking tourist exhibit!

The sounds of cheering sounded from the screens below, followed by the lady announcing a winner, but I was blocking it all out. My gut was contracting, bile in my throat, and I turned to see that the ladies had already discovered, and what now sickened me even more. There, along the sides of the wall right next to us, were more of these glass boxes. Only, the inhabitants didn't appear to see us. Maybe the walls were mirrors, or perhaps the people in them were so accustomed to being stared at. Either way, we walked past several, gawking, not getting a single reaction.

The first contained a woman, completely nude but for a loincloth, her body covered in swirling red tattoos and feathered wings growing from her arms. Her feet had talons, and her hands, claws. They'd made her into a harpy... and by my guess, this wasn't just for fighting, though she was likely good at that, judging by her muscle tone. There were more too, more that confirmed what this place was. A super whore house, but so much worse.

Orion Corp., by my guess, was using supers to genetically engineer others into perfect sex partners and fighters, all for some rich pricks' entertainment. That rhino-cocked bastard Suari had been part of it. The tunnels above, the house, all of it—it wasn't for escaping inmates or anything so noble, but for smuggling them in! Supers trafficking just like that bastard Suari with his vampire mermaid. For whatever reason, they'd had me bring in their own man. It hit me then, hard, that maybe he'd betrayed them, abandoned all of this for the love of a woman, that same woman I'd referred to as a vampire mermaid... the same whose life I'd taken. Maybe it was all in my head, or maybe I'd guessed right. Either way, Orion Corp. had to pay.

Fuck these people! Rage swelled inside me and I wanted to turn and scream, to shout how I'd kill every last one of the Orion Corp. pricks. But instead, I froze when I saw the next cell over. There, kneeling on the floor and crying, was a man with a snake for the lower half of his body. He was trying to fight the tears but simply wasn't able.

He started screaming, and then suddenly was up and slithering toward the glass, throwing himself against it, pounding—and his eyes met mine.

"This isn't going to help us get out of here," I hissed, pulling the ladies back. "If anything, they'll catch us and use us as test subjects, too."

Cheri pouted in her cute little way, seemingly wanting to stay and help the man, but Erupa nodded. "He's right, move it."

We charged back out and into the metal tunnel, and were halfway back toward the stairs that led up to the main tunnel when we heard a voice that said, "Freeze, or we shoot."

Damn, we were in deep shit now.

8

Every ounce of my being said that this couldn't be the end, not after what I'd just learned about Orion Corp. Not before I had the chance to stand on the tallest buildings and denounce them, to call for their downfall. Knowing what they were doing to people, supers or not, it wasn't right. Even the worst villains didn't deserve what we'd seen down there.

"Any doubts, now?" Erupa asked in a hoarse whisper.

I hesitated, then gave a slight shake of my head.

"Then can we kill these fucks?"

This time, a nod.

Her expression went from annoyed to devilish, and before anyone there knew what was happening, she had turned, seemingly latched onto one of the forms behind her, and then become a shadow, his shadow, where she rose up behind him, taking his pistol and shooting a hole through his head. She'd tried that move on me, but I'd been ready, previously briefed on her shadow attack method—how she could do it only when not already engaged in combat or expecting to fight, surge through the darkness and rise from her prey's shadow as she'd just done. In our case, I'd simply ensured the fight was on before she even knew I was there, swinging at the air like a madman. But hey, it had worked.

Two more men were there, both starting to turn on her as we reacted. In my rage, I had no hesitation regarding taking their lives, so I busted out my quick draw. *Bam!* The first was dead, both Erupa and Cheri already on the third. A punch from Cheri and the man fell back, a kick from Erupa and he sprawled across the floor as his gun went clattering, and I pocketed it for later.

He actually recovered, pulling a baton similar to my own but lacking electricity, and cracked it across Cheri's forearm so hard that it should've broken bone. That was all in her bounty file, and another reason for her former super name, which had been Lechas. Bones that didn't break, the rumors went.

Like too much calcium… like milk. Close to leches—or milk. Yeah, it was a stretch, hence the stories of her love of Tres Leches Cake, but changing the "e" to an "a" to be original. And she'd since changed her name to avoid always having to think of cake which she didn't have access to. According to her, it was too damn depressing.

Likewise, there was no cake here, only her grinding her teeth in anger before leaping on the man and commencing to beat the life out of him.

When she was done, she stood and, wiping the blood from her knuckles onto one of the other corpse's clothing, said, "Is that all of them?"

No alarm was sounding yet, so I nodded and started dragging the bodies out of the middle of the hallway. At least if they were in the corners, they might not get noticed. The ladies followed suit and soon we were charging back down the hall, faster now.

We reached a stairway up. It continued down the tunnel, where more guards might show up, or get out of there and work our way to the asylum above ground. We went with the latter.

I came to a realization as we climbed above. We weren't going to kill this rebel leader, because whoever it was, Orion Corp. wanted him or her dead. Instead, we were going to find allies, work on a way to hit the corporation where it hurt. Right below us, they were making money off of the elites, they were parading their abominations around and laughing behind our backs. All of it was for show, or so that we could go be little peons in their armies.

A glance over at Erupa and then Cheri, and I smiled. We weren't going to let Orion Corp. do any of that. We were going to knock them on their asses. And the best part? We were going to have a damn good time doing it.

Pushing through the top of the stairs, we saw that we were in a small building at the outskirts of the guard posts. Others nearby were completely demolished, some still smoldering, smoke blowing in the breeze at an angle. It was a cold breeze, though I had to wonder, knowing what I did of this place now, if even the weather was fabricated. Was that possible?

One trail of smoke caught my eye more than the rest because it was coming from my ship. There where I'd left it, now lying at a tilt as part of the landing gear had clearly been damaged, was my baby.

"We shouldn't go for it," Cheri said, sounding spooked. "The voices are telling me."

"The voices?" I scoffed. "Where were they down in the tunnel, huh?"

She glanced over, annoyed, and said, "It's not like I can tell them when to come or when to go."

"I'm with cop-boy here," Erupa said, pointing. "Because of that, right there."

Following her line of sight, I frowned. Lying on its side at the top of the ramp was the lantern I'd kept Tink in. What had they done to her?

"Come with or don't." I pushed my way out, moving to the doorway, and was glad to see both of them right behind me. A thought struck me. "Erupa, how—"

"Before I found you, I ran back on the ship with that big guy, the one with the scars on his face. Saw her and tried to get to her, but the mob—it was too much. I felt like shit, so it isn't going to happen again."

My response to that was a simple nod, hand moving to my baton, and then making a dash for the ship. To my surprise, no shots came my way. I leaped over a body, started down a small ditch, almost a valley, and froze—it was full of bodies, small robots with bulldozer-style sides to them busy at the far end dumping another in. Almost as if they were used to this, almost as if all of this was expected, planned for.

"Keep moving," Erupa said, flicking my ear and then leaping over the bodies, scrambling up the other side.

Cheri did the same, performing a sort of ballerina leap as she cleared it. But when I tried to follow, I stumbled, nearly fell back into the bodies, and noticed a robot turn my way, waiting to see if I belonged down there or not. A shot rang out, missed, and then Cheri was there, grabbing me by the bullet-proof vest and pulling me away from that spot.

"Told you," she said, pointing to her head. "The voices."

"Right," I replied, and then was with her, running for the ship as another shot rang out. This one hit the back of my vest, sending me sprawling.

It was a damn fine vest, so the shot barely fazed me aside from the feeling like I'd been punched in the ribcage and slightly lost my breath. I kept on, crawling up the rest of my ship's ramp, and then cut my hand. I glanced down at it, annoyed and confused, then realized why.

Glass from the lantern—it was on its side, the glass gone. What I'd thought might have been Tink was just a foot from a burnt corpse. Erupa was already there, at the top of the ramp with her newly acquired pistol at the ready, scanning the area outside.

"See if you can find anything worth taking," she said. "The fairy's gone."

"Maybe they have her inside," Cheri suggested.

"Or maybe they fucking ate her," Erupa shot back. "We shouldn't be making assumptions, and..." She cursed, pissed at herself, and there was something else there.

"Shit, you knew her," I said. "What, friends?"

Erupa nodded, curtly. "Her family got a warning out to me that you'd taken her in, and that I was next. Partly I stayed to stop you, to try and help her. But you came, and you kicked my ass, imprisoning me... and now I'm fighting at your side?"

"No," I said.

"Excuse me?"

"That wasn't me," I stated. "That was someone from another life, someone who thought he was doing the right thing. At least..." A shot rang out, hitting the spot right next to my foot and I realized I'd been standing too close to the edge of the ramp. Pulling back, I looked to her and said, "So what, all those people you hurt, killed... they were all bad?"

She nodded. "Supervillains, as dictated by the Citadel Elders."

"Bullshit." I scoffed, but then pursed my lips, brow furrowing. "What makes you so sure?"

"You want to know how I can be so certain?" She walked down to the edge of the ramp, turned, squinting, and fired. The next shot came, but a flicker of black emanated from her horns like she'd been engulfed in shadow for a split second, and the bullet struck the ramp behind her with a *twang.* She fired back, three good shots and then grinned before walking back up to me. "There, see what just happened?"

"A bullet went through you?"

She nodded. "If I know it's coming, yeah."

"I'm not following."

One of her eyes squinted more than the other, then she laughed. The laughter faded, and she was staring at the floor. Even Cheri was looking at her like she'd lost her mind. But finally, as the robots rolled past outside to deal with more of the dead, she spoke.

"It was cold, I remember that. The way cold can get where it chills your bones, like a cold wind that, no matter how many layers you wear, it still gets inside you. I was sitting around the fire with my sisters, all older, all telling stories of how they wanted to go to Supraline's like our oldest sister, who was visiting us but was with Mom and Dad at the moment, showing them what she'd learned.

"I snuck away at one point, wanting to watch. We'd already seen her show off her powers enough times, but for me it was never enough. I was so fucking proud. There I was, halfway to the courtyard when I saw the figures in the darkness, watched their blades take out my parents and then my eldest sister. There wasn't anything I could do... but when they turned for my sisters, I snapped out of it, charging back and shouting. It was the first day I learned about my ability to shadow travel, and that it only works on one in a group, or within a limited window. There's more to it, but as far as that traveling attack, yeah. I got the first, then shouted for my sisters to run as I charged a second. He already had his rifle up, aimed at me, but the bullets went right through in what I could only describe as gaps in my memory. I was running, the bullets still weren't hitting me, and then I was tearing the man apart.

"When the barrage of bullets hit and took out my sisters, I turned, horrified that I hadn't been able to save them. Two were still alive, fighting back, but bleeding badly."

She paused, arms shaking, finger moving back and forth as if about to go for the trigger.

"I—I can't imagine," I said.

"You can, but you'd have to imagine yourself in the shoes of the shooters." She looked at me with pure hatred then, her eyes almost turning red, it seemed. "They were all Orion Corp. I found out when I saw that fucking "O" on the badge when I tried to kill one, and only survived because I fell, tumbling down a cliff. Dead for sure, they must've thought, their point made."

"What point?" Cheri asked.

She took a deep breath. "None. There was no point, at least, not one that made sense to me. But I later heard it was simple—the headmistress of Supraline's had refused their request for all 'demons,' as they called us, to be sent to them for mandatory service when finishing the academy. The headmistress told them to fuck off, so my family was the response."

I gulped, only then realizing that my arms were shaking too. After what we'd seen down below, this was a shock, but it didn't surprise me anymore.

"You might hate me because of who I was," I said, slowly, trying to think through what I was saying. This could go south fast. "But believe me... that wasn't who I thought I was. This... all of this? What you're saying, what's going on here, it's totally fucked. And you want to see them fall, right? See them suffer for what they did. Me too, okay? Me. Fucking. Too."

Cheri stood there awkwardly for a minute, then held up a hand, "Me too. The voices said to just stay quiet, but… I want to be clear—me too."

"Got it," Erupa said, actually allowing a half-laugh at her. She breathed long and deep, then looked at me, making eye contact. "Cheri, what do your voices say about this guy?"

"That he fucked up. But that we're going to need him if we really want to do this. Oh, and that he's great in the sack, and that you should try him out. His sex sweat smells like a walk in the forest."

Erupa frowned. "Cheri…"

"The last stuff might have been all me," Cheri admitted. "It's hard to tell the difference sometimes."

A moment followed during which we could hear shouting from inside the compound, some clanging and banging, and then silence for a moment. The clanging started again, and Cheri said, "Maybe we should get moving?"

"Wait," Erupa still held my gaze, but now her expression was softening. "She's with you, but she's crazy. You really are this new man? Prove it, but we have to move fast. It's not like there are a lot of options here, but I want you to know that I'm choosing to stick with you, okay? To show you that

I'm not like those Orion pieces of shit, or what they tried to say my family was post-mortem, those filthy lies. Fuck! Okay?"

"Yeah," I said. "Whatever we think about each other—whatever we thought—clean slate. From now on, you're just a hot super with horns."

"And you're just a semi-attractive horny guy," she shot back. The corner of her lip curled up. "Let's go see what the hell's going on in that asylum, shall we?"

"Please," I said.

"About damn time!" Cheri said, and she bent down, daintily, holding up a grenade that apparently hadn't exploded. "Oooh, look what I found."

If that one was intact, I wondered. Turning to the side of my ship, I found a portion of the wall knocked open by a blast, but not enough for the enemy to have found my stash. Oh hell yeah, this was about to get interesting.

The explosion hadn't damaged my babies. If it had, a much larger explosion would've followed, because in here I had stashes of gear to use during my bounty hunting. Everything from flash grenades and frags, sleeping darts and powders, several more pistols, and items I'd confiscated over the years.

As soon as I realized what we had, I slammed the button in the back to see if the ramp could still close.

To my relief it did, though only about seventy-five percent of the way.

"What was that about?" Erupa asked, glancing over, her eyes going wide to see all the gear I started pulling out.

Cheri yelped at the sight of her sword and snatched it, kissing the hilt and then rubbing the teddy bear chained to the bottom. "For good luck," she explained when she saw me giving her a confused look. "And because I missed her."

"Then it all makes perfect sense," I replied with a grin. Equipping myself with an extra pistol, I had to admit I felt more at ease.

We stocked up on other gear, to include grenades and a few energy bars I'd stored in here. There were only two water pouches, enough for us each to have just enough for now. As we went through the rest of it, my empath powers on high alert in case there was a problem, I suddenly sensed very strong excitement from Erupa.

"Where the fuck did you get this?" she asked as she pulled out a wrist device, several packages of wrist and shin protectors, and other odds and ends.

"One of my targets was transporting," I said. "Not sure where to, but yeah, intercepted and didn't have a clue what it all was."

She gave me an amused glance and said, "Ezra—"

"Oh, so you do know my name."

"Shut up, and yes. This stuff… it's Citadel-level shit. Forget SupraTech, this makes you the weapon."

"I'm not following."

"Think biotech combined with nanotech but powered by superpowers. Basically, it's an augmented reality system of upgrades, based on the powers of one of two supers I know of. One of them is called Lamb and works at the Citadel. If these originated with her, we might be in for a grand ol' time."

"Holy shit," I replied, sarcastically. "I have no idea what you just said."

"Aug-Eye implants, with boosters placed in certain parts on body and weapons…" She turned to me and grinned. "Our chances of taking down this shithole just got a whole lot better."

Cheri pointed to the smiley face on her tit, as if the smile on her face wasn't enough to show how she felt about that.

"Perfect, how does it work?"

"Yeah, that's the hitch," Erupa said.

"You don't know how to work it?"

"Oh, I know. Problem is… will it work for us? See, the thing is that these kind of toys, if you will, are kind of imbued with her powers, but it's more than that. I've heard it called her essence."

"Sounds gross," Cheri said but shrugged. "Doesn't mean I'm out. Just… gross, is all."

I laughed. "So it's SupraTech."

"You're not listening." Cheri took the wrist device along with a case that held various arm guards and shin guards. "There we go… if it accepts us I mean."

"You keep saying that…"

"Right." She grimaced, then looked from me to Cheri. "We're all fighting against Orion Corp. now, agreed?"

"Yes," I said, and Cheri shrugged but then nodded enthusiastically.

"And because the Citadel is fighting Orion Corp., we're kind of on the side of the Citadel. Well, let's find out if the Citadel sees it that way."

With that, she turned to me first and started putting on the wrist piece—which had a green lit up area on it, like a screen. Then she attached some of the shoulder guards and leg gear, taking others for herself and Cheri. Oddly, as soon as they slipped them on, the gear started adapting to match whatever they were wearing. I looked down to see mine did the same.

"That's a good sign," Erupa said. Next, she closed her eyes, and said, "Here's hoping." When she opened them again, she blinked, her mouth fell open, and she grinned wider than I'd seen her yet.

"What?" Cheri asked, and tried the same. "Oh, badass."

I don't know what's happening," I admitted. "More... crazy?"

"Fuck you," Erupa said. "Just blink and wish to see your stats."

That's what I did and, sure enough, I saw what had made them so excited. First, there was a screen that showed various aspects about myself, assigning levels of skills and abilities. It told me that my strength was a seven on the scale of ten, my speed a nine, and verified me as a Tier Four super—which had always annoyed the hell out of me, but I knew it had to do with how powerful we were and therefore was valuable in some strange class sense that was bullshit. What I wondered was, were the stats starting points that could go beyond ten, or was that the max? I was guessing they could go beyond, and that excited the hell out of me.

At the bottom left, it had a line that read: *Empath. Quick Draw and Aim. Upgrade?* I reached out with my hand, confused about how to interact with these screens, but sure enough, they stayed in place and I was able to click on the upgrade option. A new window showed, with options for how my powers could be enhanced or upgraded.

"It seems to be gauging our current levels and

powers," I said. "And then... somehow it enhances us? Like an amplifier power?"

"Ezra, Ezra, Ezra," she said, moving around in her screens, though I couldn't see them. Somehow, we could each only see our own screens. "You don't seem to realize that you brought a knife to a gun fight, and all along you had the equivalent of a mech warrior with a nuclear core."

"Really fucking cool," Cheri chimed in. "Like we were getting darts thrown at our faces from the heavens, now the gods are all jizzing on our—"

"Too far," Erupa stopped her. "Know when it's too far, okay?"

"Hey, you like mechs, I like god jizz."

"Seriously, she's right," I said, agreeing with Erupa, but Cheri just shrugged and went back to her screens.

I did the same because I was fascinated. The later levels didn't give me the details of what I'd achieve, but level two mentioned being able to expand my ability to sense attacks and enhance my range. Both sounded intriguing. Nothing related to my gun handling yet, but then again I was about as good as they came at that, so it figured.

"What do your upgrades do?" I asked them.

"Isn't that a bit personal?" Erupa asked but had a hint of a smile.

"Meaning you won't tell me?"

She shrugged. "You know about my shadow strike, the one I almost used on you when you were taking me in. It's kind of all bullshit, more like giving someone a bad burn, but I built it up in stories over the years. Well... that might not have to be the case for much longer."

"No shit?"

She smiled wide this time. "We just have to live long enough to level up, and we'll find out. Also, my other skills look like they have promising upgrades."

"I'd imagine a Tier Three has plenty of badass skills," Cheri said, frowning.

"You've got your... thing," she said, glancing my way.

"Cheri can hear voices," I said, trying to talk her up, but when the words left my mouth, they didn't sound as cool as I'd hoped. "I mean—"

"And other things," Cheri said, waving off the comment and giving me a glare that I took as a sign to shut up.

"Well, anyway, this is going to kick ass," I said, making sure we had all the grenades, ammo, and blades we could handle, then making sure the rest was better hidden. We were just about to head back out when my empath power picked up on hostility.

"Whoever's in there, get your asses out here,

now!" a man's rough voice called from outside the ship.

"Guess playtime's over," Erupa said, swiping away her screens as I did the same.

"You kidding?" Cheri said, licking her lips and moving her sword around in a practiced kata form. "Playtime's just getting started."

9

We lowered the ramp and stepped out, armed to the teeth. No shots came yet, so at least they were smart enough to gauge our strength before attempting an attack. Only one man was visible, but now that I was aware of potential trouble, my empath ability was firing all sorts of warnings my way. The guy had the arrogance of a prick who had us vastly outnumbered. And now that I thought about it, did our Citadel gear do any good if we hadn't leveled up yet? Something I'd prefer not to find out, but our recent weapons find would help in that regard.

"Which side?" the man said.

"Not happening," I replied. "You first."

"No shame here. We mean to kill Muerta. Now, if you're on her team, speak up so we can kill you too.

If not, hop on over here, boy, so I can welcome you to the winning side."

"We have a problem," Erupa hissed next to my ear. "He just said Muerta."

"I heard," I replied, remembering that name all too well. I remembered the contract and remembered being pissed when Antinel was the one to bring her in. Let's see, former Orion Corp. chief, turned after... "Wait, didn't she slaughter her whole team?"

"Yes, but she even admitted it."

"You two lovebirds done chatting?" the man asked. "We've got a whole hell of a lot of people to kill, and you're slowing us down."

I didn't like the tone of this guy, and his emotions were coming across as super aggressive. As if he was actually just talking to us because he had to... to *distract* us. My gun went up and I spun at the same time Cheri did, apparently her voices telling her about the guy sneaking up behind us. The poor bastard didn't even have a chance, his leg coming into view and me shooting out his kneecap before spinning back to take out the guy with the cocky attitude.

More appeared, and now Erupa had a pistol, roaring as she charged them. It seemed like a bad move, considering the fact that the ship could provide cover and she was now out in the open. Then again, a blue lady with horns charging you and shooting can be scary. I spun to see if Cheri needed help, but she was leaping into the air with thrusters on her boots, her sword crunching down through the man's skull. She kept going, flipping over the side of the ship and landing to apparently take out another attacker, as there was a yelp and a thump. But then the gunshots started from all over.

One hit me, but the wrist device made a sound as a shield flickered around me. Now the device had a number on it, reading seventy-nine percent. It was a shield! Had Erupa knowingly given me the only shield? I'd have to talk to her about that.

In the meantime, the speaker had pulled out some sort of energy force field, a handle in his hands and shield spreading out before him, and he was backing up to a fence where others were now firing from. They'd clearly gotten one of those loot crates the Orion light-being had spoken of because these certainly weren't the guards' weapons.

The ship was providing me with some cover, shots pinging off it, but Erupa was out in the open near the attackers, and I had no idea where Cheri had gotten off to at that point. I figured my best bet was to stick with the one I could see, so shouted,

"Advance!" in case Cheri could hear me, and then charged, shooting as I went.

My shield took two more hits, causing me to stumble each time as they packed a bit of a wallop. But much better than death, at least. Forty-three percent left, I noted when reaching the gate next to Erupa.

We had a section of the wall on our side of the gate, using the base of a guard tower to fire on the enemy on the other side. Erupa gestured for me to follow, and soon we were charging up the stairs, so that we were able to fire down on the enemy who, confused about where we'd gone, had started charging around to our side of the wall. We dropped five of them before the others realized what was happening and got to cover. Next, we charged across the gate to their side, where we took out two more before descending.

"You aren't so bad for a dick," Erupa said, helping me down the last bit of the wall by grabbing on with one arm and swinging me down. Damn, she was strong—the muscles in her arms bulged, making me jealous.

I landed to find a woman swinging a machete at me, but was fast enough to duck and sweep out her legs. Erupa landed on her a second later, knocking the blade away and dealing her some damage, while I turned to fight two mangy dogs of men who were like fighting whirlwinds. They were everywhere, trying to get in any attack they could with flailing arms and legs, and after a moment of confusion, I ducked and rolled out of that shit, coming up to shoot them both in the heads. Forget fairness when they're acting like idiots.

Another exited and had a large rifle that showed a bar of charged energy on the side, but he had it aimed at me and didn't see Erupa there at his side. She frowned, assessing the gun, and then kicked out his knee before snapping his neck. As he started to fall, she reached out and took the gun, shouting, "Mine."

She spun and unleashed a beam that tore through a man charging us from behind and caused another to flee. But another shot and it started to smoke. She cursed and tossed the thing, diving back to tackle me to the ground as it exploded.

I stared up at her there on top of me, realizing her leg was pressed against my crotch and gulped. She gave me a curious look, then jumped up and helped me to my feet. Nobody was left but us.

We'd just gotten our stash of loot, but had to admit some of the weapons these bastards had were worth taking. The most impressive was a glove with odd attachments that would shoot out a burst of fire when the wearer was throwing punches. Erupa picked that up with a wicked smile. She was going to have some fun with it, I was certain.

"Where'd Cheri get off to?" I asked, sticking my head around the edge of the wall. A man was sneaking up, rifle at the ready, but moving around our ship to the other side. Likely to take out Cheri, if she was over there. I took aim and fired, then signaled. "We have to go back out for her."

"And get ourselves killed… no," Erupa protested. "We just got to cover."

More gunshots and then Cheri's crazy laughter rang out.

"Maybe so, but she's still out there, and I'm going."

Erupa growled, but took up a spot next to the wall with me and said, "I'll cover you, then you cover me."

I nodded and then took off. Two men appeared to my left, rounding the side of the main asylum building, firing. Erupa took out one, and I drew on the other, dropping him with a shot to the throat. Nasty way to go.

The ship was blocking my view of Cheri, but I had to play this smart. Charging around to the right side where it was tilted over, I stopped and signaled to Erupa to follow, and then waited for any sign of trouble from her side.

"Down!" she shouted as she charged, pistol raised, and I spun to see her shot tear a hole in a woman's jaw, then another one in the chest, bringing her down.

The woman fell, having apparently climbed up on the ship and been about to attack me, and then two more came.

"Get the fuck off!" Cheri called, and Erupa arrived at my side, both of us shooting at the two men. We charged around the side of the ship to find three more attempting to climb up, while another two were struggling to pin Cheri against the side of the stricken ship.

I shot at the ones above and then pulled out my baton, cracking one of the men holding Cheri across the back of the head. When the other turned and lunged for me, he got a blast of electricity in the face, leaving nice burn marks, and throwing him backward.

Poor bastard didn't even get a chance to scream, as before he'd hit the ground Cheri had recovered her sword and was bringing it down with his fall, slicing through his neck, so that she nearly disconnected the head.

She pulled her sword free, kissed the little teddy

bear, and then turned to me as she said, "What the fuck took you so long?"

I frowned, but then noticed a screen, blinking, and grinned at the fact that it read: *Level 2, upgrade. Amplification in process.*

"Either of you get a level up?" I asked.

"Yes, but now's not the time," Erupa replied, gesturing to the side of the building where the fighters had come from earlier. More were coming now, and it was clear we needed to get out of there if we didn't want to burn through our ammo fighting them. Many were moving back along the wall we'd been at. Others were moving into a section of the asylum that had portions of the wall missing, likely from the earlier fighting, and trying to get off shots at them from there. Shots sounded from within, and one of the fighters was falling half out of the window a moment later.

"Let them fight it out," I said, indicating the other side, where the building curved in and I figured we might be able to find more cover or a way into the building.

We charged in, listening to them shout and fire at each other, and soon we were moving through empty halls and rooms until we found what seemed to be a now-emptied armory that we could lock ourselves into. The shooting went on while we checked the back windows, one where the bars had been blown off so we could have an emergency escape if needed.

"This whole place is a shithole waiting to blow," Cheri said, checking herself for bullet holes. Finding none, she grinned and said, "But hey, we're still here."

"I think we have to take out Muerta," I said, earning glares from both of them.

"And make ourselves the target?" Erupa scoffed. "No, thank you. By the time those two groups are done out there, there won't be many left. Maybe then we move in at the last minute and stake our claim, but not before."

"There might be others who need our help," I pointed out.

Cheri shook her head. "How many of the men and women you put in here would you trust? Aside from us two, that is... and honestly, you're being really stupid doing that."

"Hey," Erupa protested.

"I'm not saying he shouldn't or that we'll betray him," Cheri said. "But it's not very smart, considering."

"True."

"I..." Honestly, I didn't know what to say to that. My powers helped, to a degree, but it was true that

Cheri was hard to read at times and they definitely had reason to want to see me without a head. "Point is, you're right. But I do. Others... the more we bring in, the larger the gamble."

"Except maybe Tink, but we don't know where she is," Erupa pointed out.

I said nothing of the fact that Tink had basically threatened to bite my dick off. That could be figured out later.

We stood listening to a couple more gunshots, then what sounded like someone calling for others to fall back.

"They're either on the run or taking a break," Erupa said. "Either way, I say we take a few more minutes, make sure they're clear, then get back to searching this place."

"Agreed," I said.

Cheri went to the window, scanning, then looked back at the two of us, her emotions sending a tingling sense of gratitude through me.

"Thanks for coming back for me out there," Cheri said, eyeing us both. "There aren't... there aren't many who would."

"You're one of us," I replied.

"He insisted on it," Erupa said, grinning my way. "Wouldn't even listen to reason."

"That so?" Cheri looked my way, a somberness to her.

I shrugged. "You'd do the same."

She nodded, and then came in, hard, pressing me against the wall as she pressed her lips to mine, her hand caressing my crotch.

"What's happening?" I said, pulling back.

"We have to wait this out," she said, nodding Erupa over. "What're we gonna do while they kill each other off, if not fuck each other's brains out?"

"I'll keep watch," Erupa said, stepping for the door.

Cheri grabbed her by the arm, shaking her head slowly. "I think we'll hear 'em if they come back this way. You're part of this now."

Erupa frowned, caught off guard by that, and then Cheri guided her by the lower back toward me. My heart was thudding, my cock stiffening, but I felt the situation was as awkward as Erupa's expression was saying.

"Listen, I really can't," she protested, but when Cheri took our heads and guided us toward each other, neither of us resisted, and a moment later, her lips were pressed against mine, moving gently, then with passion as her tongue joined in, and I was getting into it too, Cheri moving around back and reaching around to caress my chest and then down south.

My kissing grew more passionate then, and it wasn't until my pants were undone and hands were on caressing me down there that I realized there were three of them. I pulled back to see Erupa glance at me and then down, Cheri guiding her hand to caress my cock.

She held it there when Cheri moved her hands to my balls and thighs, massaging me and watching excitedly to see what would happen next. That blue hand stood out against my pale cock like a spotlight on the fact that it was happening, and when she started stroking it on her own, it was with a curiosity that was foreign to this concept, followed by an intensity only she with her strength could manage. I pulled her back in for a kiss as my body trembled from the bliss of her touch, and then Cheri was giggling, leaning into my ear and saying, "Try to keep it quiet," as apparently, I'd started moaning and not even realized it. "Now, touch her."

It wasn't like I needed direction, but when Erupa's eyes darted to mine and she looked hopeful, I was glad to oblige. Her stroking slowed as my hand found the edge of her pants, and then worked in. She had no hair down there, just the clean slit of her pussy, wet and ready.

"What—what're we doing?" she asked, her free hand grabbing my ass and pulling me close, and then I felt Cheri's mouth on my hips, kissing, moving in closer.

"Do you want me to stop?" I asked.

Erupa shook her head but glanced toward the door, clearly worried about our timing on this whole thing.

"Our powers will warn us," Cheri said, and then took Erupa's hand from my cock and put it on the back of her head, then took my cock in her mouth.

Neither of us understood at first, but then Cheri took Erupa's hand from behind and started guiding her. When she let go, Erupa's brow furrowed, but she started guiding the woman's head on her own, then was gripping her hair and really getting into it, all while my fingers found her and started banging her like it was my cock. She moved to the wall next to me so I could get a better angle, but it didn't last long this time. Before I knew it, I was shaking and then my cum was shooting down Cheri's throat, and she was loving it, Erupa finally letting loose on her hair.

Cheri sat back, swallowing, and wiped her mouth. "Now you, on her."

Neither Erupa or I knew what she meant, at first, but when Cheri flickered her tongue out playfully, I got it, now kneeling and moving Erupa's legs apart so that I could find out what blue pussy tasted like. Not surprisingly, like all other—and I was loving it. She was so smooth, I had to wonder if her superpower-related mutations had caused no hair down there. I started getting up in there, engulfing it and then going to her clit and having a field day. A thought struck me and I turned to see if Cheri was okay.

Cheri was on the floor, sitting on my vest, with her wet panties to the side, fingering herself with one hand and massaging her clit with the other.

"Don't stop," she said. "It's so fucking hot."

So I turned back to Erupa's pussy and dove in. It was like licking a juicy mango that squirmed a lot, and I just kept on going, imagining what else I'd like to do to that mango. Soon there was a heavy but muffled moaning, then "mango juice" everywhere. *A squirter*, I thought as I wiped my chin and smiled. *Nice.*

"There, now we're cum sisters," Cheri said between deep breaths. She slid her fingers out and let her panties fall back into place, then laid there a moment longer.

"Sure," Erupa said, eyes closed and grinning. "Call it whatever you want, as long as we get to do this again."

"Definitely."

"Um," I spoke up, really not wanting to ruin this but very confused. "Whatever just happened, you... neither of you has a problem with it?"

Erupa looked from me to Cheri, then back to me. "It was fun. So... no."

"She's a Psychobitch now," Cheri said as if that explained everything. "One of us, through and through."

Erupa's eyes met mine, and as much as I thought she'd protest or be annoyed at the title, she simply smiled and held my gaze. So she was one of us, I realized, but also knew it was time to move on now.

"Come on," I said to the two. "I think we've waited long enough."

"If I can walk," Erupa said with a hushed laugh. "That tongue of yours..."

I blushed as Cheri walked past, whispering, "I'll want to feel it next time," and then went to the door to have a look around. It had been a while since I'd had a chance to hang out with any women, but I couldn't imagine the majority of them acting like this. Then again, would most men act as I had? Who was I kidding, of course every man I'd ever known would jump at the chance for two ladies... though some would have issues with the blue skin and horns, or be wary of the fact that very recently both women would've been happy to kill me.

Well, fuck all that. I was having fun and it felt right. My empath abilities were sending me good feelings from these ladies, and their smiles and the warmth in my dick all spoke toward not backing down. Allowing logic into the mix would just screw it all up.

Cheri glanced back and gave us a nod. At least at the moment, no shots were being fired. It took Erupa and me an extra couple of minutes to be ready, but then we were all up and moving through the dark passage, ready for whatever was to come next.

We snuck through the halls of this offshoot of the asylum, very aware that at any moment someone could pop up with a gun or weapon of some sort and we'd have no idea whether to shoot them or shake their hand. A change had come over Erupa since the room back there, and every time I glanced back, she would give me a bashful smile. It was so weird, so not her.

On the fourth time, I slowed and said, "Is... I don't know. Is everything okay?"

"I can't stop remembering the feeling of your tongue in me," she whispered. "So warm, soft... gentle." She leaned in. "Next time I want something not soft, not gentle."

I chuckled and glanced around. "Shouldn't we be focused here?"

She shrugged. "I'm focused... on your cock."

Cheri turned on us, a finger to her mouth. "You want the whole place to think we're a bunch of horny teenagers?"

"Aren't we?" I said. "I mean, acting like it."

"Nothing wrong with a healthy appetite for cock or pussy," she countered. "But the rest of the world doesn't know that. Erupa, pull yourself together."

Erupa stared as if she'd just been slapped. The tough, demon-looking lady had just been told to pull herself together by this self-proclaimed Psychobitch with blue pigtails, and that got to her.

"Sorry, won't happen again," Erupa said, brushing past us and taking the lead.

"Ugh." Cheri glared at me as if that was my fault. "You don't have to not let it happen again," she told Erupa, "just know the moments. I'm batshit crazy, right?" She jogged up, catching Erupa by the arm. "Right?"

"Sometimes I think so," Erupa said, spinning. "Others, I'm not so sure."

"Right, because I pick my moments."

"So you're not really crazy?"

"No!" Cheri winked, then turned to me and held up her fingers like counting down from three, then pointed my way and waited.

"Oh, right," I said. "Not crazy, psycho."

"Okay, so you're not really psycho, I mean," Erupa asked. "It's an act?"

Cheri thought about that a moment, then said, "Depends, doesn't it? If you mean do I have no control of my brain whatsoever, the answer's no. I don't not have control. But if you think I'm normal, that would make you an idiot, right? I do whatever the fuck I want, when I want, and don't exactly view the world the same way everyone else would. Does that make me a tad loopy?" She shrugged. "Who the fuck cares, I'm having fun."

Erupa considered this a moment, then said, "What you're saying is, enjoy the head, crave the fuck, but... not when we could get killed at any minute and should be paying attention?"

"That'd be a good start."

"Sounds like something I should be saying to you," she said, taking her pistol and motioning us on, now doing a better job of checking each new hallway. "You have to understand... getting laid or head or whatever... it's not easy when you look like me."

"What, why?" Cheri asked. "You're hot?"

"Come on." Erupa glanced back, but Cheri seriously looked like she didn't understand. "Ezra, explain."

"I—" I started, but Cheri saved me.

"If he's about to say some bullshit about the blue skin or horns, fuck that. I was serious before, and he's going to love it—Ezra, when she goes down on you, and she will, grab those horns and fucking own it. It'll be like you're driving this dick-sucking machine, right?"

Erupa blushed but didn't protest or say she wouldn't like that. In fact, she was looking at me out of the corner of her eye and then returning to check for enemies.

"And the blue skin—"

"It's hot," I interrupted her this time.

"Yeah?" Erupa asked.

"Anyone who thinks skin that's blue, green, orange, whatever isn't hot is either prejudiced or just stupid. I'm not saying regular skin tones aren't sexy too, I'm just saying it's like when you have two guys, one's eyes are bright blue and the other's green. You might look at each and think they're both sexy in their own way, right? And then you have brown, and you can stare into a woman's brown eyes and think they're just as beautiful or enticing… I don't know if I'm getting this across, but what I'm trying to say is that it's more than all that, it's what's beneath. And if I'm looking at any color of eyes on the right woman, I'm drawn in. Same way with your skin."

"Deep," Cheri said, rolling her eyes. "Me? I just

think his pale dick would look hot going in and out of your blue pussy. But I'm an artist when it comes to sex, so I can appreciate the contrast in colors, the juxtaposition and all that." She grinned wide, and I wasn't exactly sure what to think about her statement, but then she added, "That's why I dyed my hair like this, so if I'm ever going down on a guy, he can think of the great feeling of my mouth on him but also remember cotton candy and everything fun in life," and I couldn't help but laugh out loud.

I instantly put a hand over my mouth, suddenly remembering the need for silence, and we stood there, listening, but neither Cheri nor I picked up anything with our powers.

"You want men to think about cotton candy when you're going down on them?" I asked.

"What would you want a lady to think about?" she countered. "The boring wall... your thinning hair? Come on, nothing says joy like cotton candy, and when I'm bringing you to your bliss point, I want you there in every sense of the word."

For some reason, I saw an image of her in a field of cotton candy, spinning naked with her tongue out and the cotton candy flowing into her, and her eyes rolling back as she orgasmed. It took a second to realize that the emotion causing that image was coming from her, and then see the way her eyes were fluttering as she imagined something—maybe exactly that.

"Um, Cheri, maybe we didn't all have the same cotton candy upbringing you did," Erupa said. "Me, for example—I equate it with sticky fingers and an aching stomach."

"Hmmm, well, if I ever go down on you, you'll just have to think of something else then."

With that, Cheri held up a hand for silence, then crept to the end of the hallway. Erupa and I shared a look, and I couldn't help but think she was imagining Cheri going down on her just like I was. Damn, that would be hot. For some reason I'd never considered it to be before, as I wasn't into the idea of women who didn't want me involved. But with these two? Fuck yeah.

An emotion hit me, not my own or one of these two women's, but somewhere, nearby. I sensed what Cheri was going after—a woman. Not fear, not anger... curiosity?

"Don't attack," I said, and moved up close to Cheri, my currently out of control mind unable to ignore the way she was crouching and how it made her ass stick out so sexily. "Where?"

She pointed, and I looked around the corner to see the face of an attractive woman staring at me. This woman wore a revealing vest held together with mesh, tight camo shorts, and had the left side of her hair shaved in a way that made the blonde hair hanging over to the other side seem more special. There was something familiar about her, like we'd met before, but I couldn't quite place it.

"Don't move," she said, stepping out, guard rifle aimed right at us. Lying at her feet was a corpse, but not that of a guard. It was a large man who, judging by the piece of metal pipe covered in blood next to his caved-in skull, had been beaten to death with it.

I still didn't sense aggression, so stepped forward, putting my weapons away. With my quick draw, it wasn't like I was at a huge disadvantage anyway.

"You're not with the rest of them?" I asked.

She shook her head. "Judging by your conversation, neither are you."

How much had she heard? That was potentially— no, it was definitely—embarrassing. "We..." I tried to think of what to say.

"Hey, no judgment in that regard," she said with a nod to Cheri. "I've had my share of fun, believe me. But…" She saw Erupa for the first time now, and her eyes went wide. "Sorry, I just… I've heard about others like you, but never seen…"

"A freak?" Erupa said.

"No, sorry. Sorry." The woman lowered her gun,

and then stepped forward, sticking out her hand for me to shake. "I'm Letha, from Earth."

I shook her hand, introduced myself and Erupa, then Cheri. "Huh, Letha, Cheri… I hope this doesn't get confusing."

"You let it confuse you, I'll smack you upside your head," Cheri said with a laugh. "So, sugar tits, who're you?"

"Sugar…?" Letha chuckled. "I missed this kind of weirdness. I was a prisoner here, but am on the way out. Truth be told, and since I have no idea which side you're on—fight me if an enemy, help me if not—I was on my way to take out some corporation sons of bitches. Highly involved in the overthrow of my family and stealing some of my most precious memories. I mean to have my revenge."

"Revenge against the corporations isn't bad," Cheri said with a shrug.

Letha nodded, looking us over, and then said, "But I just need out of here. No offense, Ezra, you're hot as fuck and all that, but I've had enough of these scenarios to last a lifetime. No dick, no pussy… just revenge. Can you all help with that?"

I blinked, confused, and then it hit me. "Oh, shit. Letha? As in… didn't you ascend from Planet Kill?"

"What?" Erupa asked, and Cheri looked equally confused.

"Some show they get here," I said. "Caught a few streams while I was dropping off inmates from time to time. Not my cup of tea, killing and fucking and all, but this lady here was a bit of a celebrity."

Letha nodded. "Had my own harem, ascended... and then killed some important people. Tried to kill more, and ended up here."

"So she's legit?" Erupa asked.

"I'd guess so," I replied. Glancing around, I said, "Are we in trouble here? What about Muerta?"

She shrugged. "Should be fine for a bit. Saw a group of them going off to a fight. As for Muerta, she ran into some trouble and took off, chased by this group of supers, one with a tail and ears. I wasn't sure if it was a costume or for real, but now..." She faced Erupa. "...seeing you..."

"So we don't need to kill her, or at least, not unless she returns after having killed that other team."

"But there are still those loyal to her, those who—"

"DOWN!" Cheri shouted, tackling me as a strange sound hit the air and a second later...

KA-BOOM! The walls a few cells over blew inward, stone flying our way, and Letha took a strike to the shoulder that knocked her sideways. She recovered and then was up and shouting for us to get back as she charged toward the opening in the wall, shooting at some enemy she apparently saw out there.

Us get back? She clearly had no idea who we were. Cheri was the first up, then Erupa and they were both firing now, but then Cheri flung herself out through the gap!

"Holy shit," I muttered, running to the opening to see another blast coming our way from what was a sort of makeshift cannon the enemy seemed to have constructed out of various loot crate items.

I guessed that Orion Corp. had seen me out there fighting against the very same people who had proclaimed to be after Muerta's head, and now they were pissed. That also meant going on from here was going to be more of a challenge, and that if I didn't play my cards right, they might come after me directly instead of trying to have me taken out for their live event.

Which meant I needed to become a 'fan favorite' at least for a few minutes, so there'd be outrage if there was any outside interference.

Cheri had rolled and taken cover behind a half-wall, sword in hand but no guns—which pissed me off. If she could make the fall, you can bet your ass I could too.

"You all coming?" I asked and then ran out,

drawing as I did and shooting out the main cannon operator and hitting the shoulder of the guy to his left, then leaping to join Cheri.

She turned to see me coming and let out a "Woohooo!" and, emboldened by my decision, charged out from her cover to go take on the enemy. Since the cannon shooter was down and the other guy injured, that gave her a window as the enemy was working to get their fancy weapon back in place.

I hit hard but rolled into it as I'd practiced numerous times back in my training at the temple. There was something else at work in my landing though, as it seemed to go much smoother than I'd anticipated. When I was up, I remembered leveling up and wondered if somehow that had something to do with it. No time to check now, though. The two ladies above were on their way down, lowering themselves instead of jumping, and I needed to provide cover fire for them as well as for Cheri.

Sure enough, a new operator was at the cannon and they had it aimed in at Cheri. It would tear a fucking hole in her, and that would certainly ruin my day. So this time I aimed from a still position, letting my full instinct take over, and shot. The bullet went true, straight in through the end of the cannon, blowing them the fuck up.

It was a nice fireworks show, metal exploding and flames erupting, then the three enemy fighters running about on fire. What made it more dazzling was when Cheri was in among them, slashing and thrusting, separating a head here and gutting another there, and then her teddy bear caught fire and it was swinging around like she was putting on a fire show.

Cheri being Cheri, the moment she saw this she fell to the ground, snuffing out the fire on her bear and screaming, "Man down! Man down!"

It was a fucking teddy bear, but I cared for her so the first thing I did when reaching her side was kneel, check on the bear—only half-singed—and tell her the bear was going to make it.

She smiled amid tears, and then we were up together charging into the enemy once more.

A few had seen what we'd just done and retreated to regroup, but just then another group arrived, staring in confusion from the original group to us. Making up their minds, they charged us. These guys didn't have any guns so that meant hand-to-hand, which suited me just fine.

"This'll be fun," Cheri said, voicing my thoughts exactly.

I stowed my pistol and drew the arc baton, charging in at Cheri's side. Shots rang out from behind and three of the first line fell, trampled by their companions. Then we were in the mix, Cheri's sword slashing in one direction, my baton going to work in the other. This was where the adrenaline kicked in, where I started to feel like a true Psychobitch, laughing like a madman as a punch struck me across the ribs and a giant of a man tried to lift me up so he could slam me head-first. I managed to get my baton around and zap him full of electricity, which also hit me, but at least it got me out of his clutch. I recovered before him and came in with a push kick to the face that flattened his nose and sent blood gushing. I turned to my next opponent as Cheri brought her sword down through the area between the man's shoulder and neck.

Erupa roared as she charged into the fight, horns taking out a man and claws ripping through another, and then I spun to crack my next foe across the jaw with my baton. The newcomer, Letha, was there, watching us with fascination and curiosity, but smiled at my glance and then stepped in to help out, using her rifle as a weapon to break skulls.

I saw Cheri get knocked back. A woman had her by the hair, yanking her and dragging her across the ground as a man stepped up with a sledgehammer ready to bring down on her face. Erupa saw it too and did her shadow kill thing, reappearing behind him to yank away his hammer and spin so that when he turned to see what had happened, the hammer crushed his face instead.

Cheri finally managed to reach up and grab her opponent's wrists, then kicked up to land her boot in the woman's face, just as I got there to finish the job with my baton.

"Next time, feel free to use your pistol," Erupa said to me.

Cheri, still recovering, waved off the comment and said, "No, fuck that. Takes away from the excitement."

"Speaking of excitement…" I pointed to our new friend, who was going bare-knuckle with a woman and man, all by herself, and doing quite well.

"I'll even the odds," Erupa said, already taking off.

"They looked even to me," I said with a chuckle.

Cheri reached over and took my hand, and I wrapped an arm around her so that we stood there like that, watching them beat the shit out of their opponents.

"The bear," she said, looking at me with the most honesty I'd ever seen in those eyes, "it's not like… I mean, I know she's not alive."

"Yeah?" I was hesitant to go anywhere near this topic.

She nodded. "But the voices, you know? It's nice

to pretend they come from somewhere, and for me that somewhere is Lilly here."

"Lilly," I said, smiling and wincing as Erupa tore the enemy woman's neck out as Letha finished off the other. "It's a nice name."

"She picked it." Cheri ran her finger along the singed part of her bear, then looked up with determination. "Let's find the rest of them, make them pay."

I agreed and helped her up so that we could finish killing everyone.

11

A s we all charged after the retreating team, Letha told us how she'd one day thought she might be able to live a normal life, to get her revenge and move on, but every step of the way she was learning more about the corporations and what had happened to her. She had become aware that there were more people than she had at first thought behind an attack on her once-wealthy family, that the heads of the corporations were behind it all. In her heart, she knew that it would likely be her end in taking them down.

"You won't be doing it alone," I told her.

"No?"

"Ezra here's a recent convert," Erupa said. "Used to serve the devil, now he means to destroy Hell itself."

"Or die trying," I said, giving Letha a nod. Maybe I didn't know the half of what she was going through, but it was my duty to see that others didn't suffer like she had, or like those we'd seen down below were still suffering.

"I believe the other team I met is going after them too," Letha said. "Maybe at this rate, I'll get there and there will be nobody left to kill."

I laughed. "What would you do then?"

She ran, focusing on her breathing, but looked confused at the question. "Hadn't thought about it," she finally said, as we reached another wall that led to a back compound of the asylum. "Maybe I come find you all and see what this world of foxy-eared and blue-skinned horned people is like?"

Erupa chuckled at that. "Not so many of either type, but you're welcome anytime. Hopefully we'll have our shit squared away by then, too."

"Problems at home?"

"More than you would believe." Erupa turned my way, an eyebrow raised. "And more than he has any idea about."

I kept my mouth shut, knowing she was right. Up to now I'd spent all of my energy on my policing work, only to find out it was all a sham. Right now I couldn't even begin to think about the greater issues in our galaxy. It was all beyond my understanding.

"Suffice it to say," Erupa continued, "an outside force has attacked, somehow Orion Corp. might be involved, and last I heard the Citadel—where the main supers hold the defense—has fallen."

We stopped now, guns drawn and checking around corners as we moved between smaller buildings of brick and stone.

"I don't follow," Letha admitted. "Supers?"

"As in, what we are," Erupa explained. "Many, many years ago colonists went into other galaxies, one being ours—and the sun mutated us, at least we think that's what did it, giving some of us superpowers."

"Holy shit, that's awesome." She shrugged. "I mean, I've seen a few things here... so that makes sense of it all, actually. But if I went there?"

Erupa and I shared a glance, both of us confused.

"You might explode," Cheri said, grinning, "or suddenly learn to fly and have lasers shooting out of your tits. Who knows."

We all laughed at that, though Letha's laugh was clearly one of confusion and concern. She didn't get Cheri like we did. Not yet.

We paused, and I asked. "You're here by yourself?"

"No," Letha said. "At least, I didn't come by myself. My companions though, I don't know. I've been looking for them since the uprising started, with no luck. I'm starting to get worried."

"We had another," Erupa said, then held her hands about six inches apart, vertically. "About this tall. Little lady, with wings."

Letha's eyes went wide. "No… a super? Others were talking about her, said they saw Orion Corp. workers taking her and a couple of others below ground. I honestly believed they were talking out of their asses."

"Afraid not," Cheri replied, then turned to me. "We have to get her—she's your responsibility."

"As were the others," Erupa chimed in. "But Flyer, or Tink, a tad more in trouble if her powers aren't working."

"I delivered…" I started in my defense, but the look of horror that came into her eyes and anger in Erupas's made me back off of that real fast. "…her, so of course I will find her."

"We," Letha said. "If there's a way to fight Orion Corp., I'm in."

"Then it's settled," Erupa said. "We take out these fucks here, and then get back down there."

"Back?"

"We might have stumbled across one of their entrances," I explained, glancing up as I remembered that all of this could be being filmed and recorded.

As if reading my mind, Letha lowered her voice as she said, "Then we need to get down there, now."

"Actually, I agree," Erupa said. "Just..." She took one of my grenades, and then I saw why. Someone had just peeked over the rooftop of a building nearby, and then there was a flash of a gun. We all took cover as Erupa lobbed the grenade.

"Where from here?" Letha asked, interrupted by a loud explosion and shouts of pain.

I turned, trying to get my bearings, and then spotted the location we'd come up through. "Follow me."

The four of us ran for the entry point to the tunnels below, only to have layers of light shine down, indicating a beacon that was traveling right along with us above our heads like a big 'X marks the spot.' It read *BONUS LOOT*.

"That can't be good," Letha said, preparing her rifle.

It definitely wasn't good because it meant that Orion Corp. certainly was aware of us and our new goal, and that now any fighters not currently engaged in the action would be coming after us. If they failed, there was no doubt in my mind that the corporation itself would come after us.

"Good?" Cheri countered, "This will be great!"

"More fun, right?" Erupa asked with a roll of her

eyes, and we all pulled up short as a new group of attackers appeared ahead, directly in our path.

As they started trying to take us out, my shield took a couple more hits but showed up starting at one hundred percent again. That meant it had a recharge function, likely based on time. I was glad for that! We were shooting, clearing a path, and going from cover to cover.

When we saw that route wasn't working, we doubled back and found one that took us over to the trees. But to get there, we still had to take out another handful of former inmates and another group that came at us dressed in dark suits of armor, suits that I assume revealed them to be some of the Orion Corp. military trainees.

Erupa used her shadow technique to appear behind one of them and then tear out her throat, then spun to use her upgraded shadow punch on the next, basically sending this one's head into a smoldering heap as the brain likely burnt up inside of his skull. Nasty—and no wonder she was Tier Three instead of four like Cheri and me. We were both badasses in our own right and knew how to work it, but the potential in Erupa was intimidating by comparison.

Her look added to the effect and scared off two more of our opponents, but they didn't make it far before being dropped by shots from me. Meanwhile, Cheri was in there tearing them down, and Letha had as good a spot to shoot as she could when not worried about friendly fire.

"Go!" I shouted when we'd made a clearing, and we moved toward the tree line, where the tracker lights had a harder time staying on us.

We were charging back in the direction we'd come, when the man from my ship, Brock, I think his name was, appeared before us with a pistol in one hand and a long knife in the other. He still had the burn marks from the bars on his face, and they were getting pussy. Nasty.

"Traitors!" he shouted at my companions, then came for me.

Cheri charged over, intercepting him before he could reach me, but the guy was fast. Now that he was in range, he was able to use his powers too, so I quickly flipped the Quencher to Mode 1, not wanting that. If I remembered correctly, he was the fucker who'd almost taken me out with this strange effect he had with his weapons that made replicating strikes—he thrust with one blade, it was like blades shooting out of it in an arch, and same with bullets, so that his range and area of attack was multiplied.

As far as I was concerned when he was armed, we had a better chance against him if he didn't have his replicating power available, although of course that meant we didn't have our powers, either. He struck, hopeful, but fell short and Cheri's sword was coming straight at him. Not fast enough, though, because he spun and shot. Luckily, the bullet went wide. The downside of his having this power was that because he relied on it he'd never become very good with his aim, and I'd been counting on that. Now I had my chance to get him, albeit without the use of my quick draw advantage. I charged in, hoping my training would be enough.

This guy was tough, and even with the dreadful burns on his face a punch to his jaw left me stumbling back in pain. Much like Tink being in her shrunken form or Erupa always being blue with horns, certain inherent powers stayed with a super when the Quencher was in effect. In Brock's case, I was guessing he had a steel skull or something of the like I'd never heard of. Probably why he'd thought he would be able to headbutt his way out through the bars back on my ship.

And now he had his knife coming down at me, and I was too dazed to do anything but stare at it. Lucky for me, I had three hardcore women at my side. Erupa knocked him sideways, and Cheri was there to slash with her sword. He was quick, pulling back so that it only caused a gash to his shoulder, but it was enough to render the knife hand useless. He lifted the gun to fire, but now it was Letha's turn.

A shot rang out and hit his other shoulder, so that he fell back cursing, then had to roll as Cheri pursued with her sword. Shots rang out, hitting the trees nearby and one even connecting with the blade to knock it from her hands. Cheri cursed and jumped for it, saving herself from another shot in the process.

By the time she recovered it, I was shouting that we needed to move, and we were off, going in a different direction than we'd started out in. We hoped to throw them off our path, and since the foliage was denser in this direction, it seemed to be working. After a few minutes of running, there were no more shots our way.

We'd lost them.

Even more exciting was the fact that after a bit of exploring and trying to figure our direction based on where we'd seen the earlier tunnel lead, we finally caught a glint of metal in the hill to our left.

We'd found another compound built into the hill, and threw ourselves into it, glad to be back inside.

12

W e figured that since this little hideout in the ground was so similar to the one we'd stayed at before, it might also have a connection to the tunnels below. While the ladies searched, Erupa reminded me this might be a good chance to check out my recent level-up, as we needed to ensure we were at our best possible ass-kicking potential down there.

I pulled up my screen, still kind of freaked by the whole idea, and scanned my stats to see that they were indeed higher. Strength was now eight, and others increased as well, but what really interested me were the powers. I selected the powers section, this time hitting the upgrade option.

It then let me choose between my powers— empath or quick draw. Honestly, I thought my ability with the pistol was better than that of anyone I'd ever met. While upgrading it certainly had its appeal, as I could always get better, it was my empath power that I'd always wanted to improve. Years spent at the temple taught me to fight, but no matter how much I'd focused on meditation and reaching out to my surroundings, I'd always felt limited.

Selecting that power now, the upgrade was confirmed and then the display read: *Expanded reach, better sensing of aggression.*

The image then faded. That was it? I guess level two upgrades weren't supposed to be mind-blowing, but still, I had kind of wanted more. I supposed it just meant I'd have to work twice as hard to get some more levels and see where it took me.

Still, better sensing of aggression sounded great, as long as the range of my Quencher allowed it. With the weapons some of these bastards had, I doubted my range would be super useful unless we managed to turn off the planet's Mega Quencher.

Thinking about this reminded me that my Quencher was set to Mode 1, so I turned it back to Mode 2 to allow my powers to work here.

"Done," I said, seeing Erupa approaching.

"Haven't found it yet," she reported, going to the door and peeking through the crack before closing it again. "You take a look around. I want to play around with my latest level-up."

I walked around, glancing at the corners and edges of walls, thinking it odd that the ladies hadn't been able to find anything yet. If they hadn't, how could I? As I searched, a thought hit me. They knew we were coming, so probably had some sort of security set up below. They wouldn't have the whole place on lockdown, not with the elites in there. They wouldn't want to risk putting out a bad name for themselves like that.

Cheri approached, talking to her bear and tapping her sword on the walls. I took her by the shoulder and held up a finger for silence. Beside her, Letha watched me with an arched eyebrow, waiting.

I closed my eyes, focusing, and it was instant— fuck yeah! It was like I could trace a fading light to where, down and to the left, a group of aggressors was moving in, preparing for an attack. Orion Corp. had likely sent security teams to each entry in the vicinity, not certain which one we'd arrive at.

Turning with my eyes open now, I could barely see the light, like sunspots but in a line, and it led to a section of the room that had a metal wall marked with lines running vertically in several spots.

Erupa entered with a broad grin, about to brag about her new upgrades I guessed, but she saw me with hands pressed against the wall and waited, anxiously. Sure enough, when I pushed against the section where the last bits of light showed the way, it moved back and then swung in. Behind it was a hole with a laser sight just starting to swivel up. Lucky me, my quick draw was faster and that idiot with the laser gave me a target.

BAM! I connected and already had one of my grenades at the ready—a flashbang, not the type to cause too much chaos. I dropped it in and spun, holding out my arms and hissing, "Look away," so that the ladies knew what was happening.

When it went off, Erupa was the first past me, vanishing into the darkness. A scream sounded a second later, cut off by a wet death choke, and then Cheri was in, rolling to the side and going to work with her sword. It didn't matter what these bastards had brought to the fight. It wasn't helping them.

Letha and I followed, saw one of them running in the darkness and heard him turning on his comms. Letha said, "Allow me," aimed and dropped him.

"Not bad," I admitted.

"Lots of practice."

I nodded, checking to ensure that the ones Erupa and Cheri had gone for were dead, and then we checked their gear for loot. We found a couple of pairs of night-vision goggles which we figured could come in handy, and of course, their rifles. One had smart grenades on him, and the chubby one had a bottle of water and some candy bars. We split those up and each took a chug of the water, then got a move on.

"There'll be more," Letha said. "Especially if they try to check in with this group and don't get a response."

"And we'll be ready for them," Erupa said with a chuckle.

"Good upgrade, then?" I asked.

"Not so different from yours, I'd imagine, but still —before I could only do the shadow kill if they weren't aware of me. Now it says I should be able to perform the move even if they are, though it has a lower success rate."

"Still, badass," Cheri said, swiping up her screens and moving her hand about in the air, then selecting something. "My turn, bitches. Ohhh yeahhh."

"What'd you get?" I asked.

"Looks like I had an ability I wasn't so aware of," she said, grinning. "It's called, according to this— grip. Like, chances of me dropping my sword were much less than others... and maybe it helped in bed?" She winked my way, then laughed. "But now, it's more than that. Said I can pull on objects, like..." She glanced around, spotted my pistol, and reached out her hand. I held on tight but felt it spin around to her like a magnet.

"Oooh, like *accio*... er, never mind," Letha said. "Shit, so... let me get this... you're not only supers, but you're able to upgrade your skills as well?"

"It's all connected to one superhero's power," Erupa explained. "She's able to grant this through items, and it works in a way that's like, it doesn't trust you at first, doesn't know if you're worthy, so the more you work with it and it's connected to you, the more you can upgrade."

"And if you use your powers for evil?" Letha said, her expression looking like she was joking, but a hint of seriousness in there.

"That's actually a good question," Erupa admitted. "But... let's not test it to find out."

"Agreed," I said, then felt my pistol get yanked out of my hand to fly across the tunnel and land in Cheri's.

"Ha, got it!" she said, beaming.

I held out my hand and she gave it back. "Sorry, but... pretty cool, huh? I mean, now if I drop my sword, not to worry."

"But the real question," Erupa said, "is have you found a use for it sexually yet?"

Cheri pursed her lips in thought, leaving a few moments of silence for us to focus on the path ahead. I was using my empath powers and not finding any sign of the enemy yet, but the tunnel was a long one, with several offshoots along the way. Red and blue lights shone out in a warm glow from the edges where the walls met the floor in places, giving the metal panels an eerie sense of some sort of police hell.

"You all have really been down here?" Letha asked.

"Through a different tunnel, but yes," I replied. "And… be ready."

She scoffed. "You'd be surprised at what I've lived through…"

"But you hadn't seen supers, or my kind before, correct?" Erupa said.

"Until I saw the one with the fox ears and tail, that's right."

"Yeah…" Cheri chimed in. "You might be in for a shock here, lady."

Letha furrowed her brow but didn't argue further. We walked on for a while, passing a side route that might have led to the place we'd been before, but it was hard to tell down here. It was the opposite direction to where we figured the entrance should be, though, based on my sense of direction. As a bounty hunter who'd spent lots of times in strange places, I'd learned to hone said sense of direction, so figured it was worth putting our bets on.

"Before," I said, slowing and glancing around, "the only reason we found our way in was because we followed others. Cheri, think your power can be used to find secret doors?"

"Like, try pulling on the walls and see if any budge?" She shrugged. "Worth a shot."

As we went, the actions caused little bursts in several spots, but they were only making screws and paneling rumble, nothing more. She stopped at one point, hand rubbing the teddy bear chained to her sword, and she tilted her head, likely listening to voices.

"I don't think it's going to work," she said, but then pointed. "But I think the door is right around here."

"A person," I said, sensing an emotion. "Yes, scared."

"Could be one of the test subjects," Erupa pointed out.

"It could be, but... all by itself?" She frowned at that, glanced around, and said, "You're thinking it's up to me, right?"

Actually, the idea hadn't occurred to me until she said it, but then I was curious. "Can your powers take you through walls?"

"Not through," she said. "But since I use the shadows or darkness, as long as there's an opening, in theory… yes."

"And if it's a cell with a crazy monster?" Cheri asked. "Is it worth the risk?"

I had a hard time answering that, so was relieved when Erupa said, "Considering we do this or Orion Corp. goes on unchecked… and we likely die anyway, I'd say we don't have a choice."

"Fuck." Cheri pulled up her teddy bear and nodded. "Fine. Lilly agrees."

That earned her a confused look from Letha, but she quickly hid the expression, apparently a fast learner.

"We're really doing this, then," Erupa said, standing tall and trying to look brave, though every sense of emotion coming from her spoke of worry.

I stepped up, a hand on her lower back, the other on her shoulder. "You got this. I'll guide you."

"Nice and gentle," she said with a forced smile. "It's my first time and all… through a wall."

It was hard not to laugh at that, but I was here to offer comfort, so I stepped aside, focusing on the emotions again until I could see the light guiding me. Damn, these level-ups were awesome.

"Here," I indicated, voice hushed. "And… veer off to the right, slightly."

"Do I kill it?" she asked, voice cracking slightly.

We all looked at each other, none of us sure how to answer that at first.

"If it's one of their soldiers, you have to," Cheri said. "A regular employee... at least knock him out, or he might raise the alarm."

"And if he comes to?" I asked.

"Fuck," Erupa said. "I mean, if they work here they know what's going on, which means they're complicit."

"So yeah, death," Cheri said. "But if it's a monster...?"

"Set it free?" I suggested.

"Might be brainwashed, confused," Erupa pointed out. "Might try to kill us as soon as run for freedom or join our fight."

"Get in there, try to not pay attention to what it is, and go unseen," Letha said. "Then none of this matters. Just find the door and open it so that we can get a move on."

"If that's an option, I'll go for that," Erupa said, and took my hand, giving it a quick squeeze before moving on, standing next to the wall, and saying, "Here goes."

Darkness took over, surrounding her, then engulfing her. She was gone, a shimmer in the darkness near the wall and then I was able to see a second emotional light but much darker. The fright of the first one peaked suddenly, then went out completely, leaving only Erupa. Then she was out of range, and we were left staring at a metal wall, not knowing what could be happening to her.

We waited long enough that we were all shifting, starting to think the worse. Cheri cleared her throat, looked about to say something, and then pursed her lips in thought. After another moment, she stepped up next to me, taking my hand in hers and pressing our bodies together. Honestly, I needed it as much as she did. I felt responsible, and if anything happened to Erupa, I don't know how I'd live with myself. Then again, it might not be a long life in that case, anyway.

"She's going to be fine," Letha said, her voice barely audible. Ironic, coming from her, since she was the only one of us standing there who didn't have special powers that helped her know things like this.

But we accepted it, hoping for it to be true.

A wall rattled ahead, not far off but enough of a distance that my Quencher wasn't offsetting the planet's Mega Quencher. We all tensed, emotions of worry and excitement coming from the ladies. I had both pistols at the ready, eyes fixed on that spot.

Another rattle of the wall, and then there was a

clang and it was open, Erupa stumbling out. She was grinning, blood on the claws of her right hand.

"Guard," she said. "Or, he was supposed to be guarding. Caught him whacking off to this." In her left hand was a small expandable screen which she tossed over.

I caught it and immediately wished I hadn't seen what was on the screen—a woman whose lower half was like an octopus, her tentacles helping her cling to a wall as several of her black, octopus arms penetrated men who yelped with pleasure.

"Sick fucks," I said.

"Who are you to judge?" she replied with a wink but then frowned. "Of course, if she's one of their prisoners... then yeah, sick fucks." She glanced down at her bloody hand and tilted her head, then added, "Glad I killed him then, especially if that's true."

I swiped the screen to get rid of the tentacle porn, came across various other options, including something that looked like a large, hairy man with huge feet, various forms of human animals, and even a mermaid going down on bathers. Deleting all available, I was about to toss the thing when I noticed a beeping on my wrist that said, "Download data?"

Maybe this thing wasn't just for porn, I thought,

so clicked out and found parent menus, including one with maps.

"Holy shit," I said, then hit the accept button on my wrist device before tossing the little computer to Cheri. "Maps."

She frowned. "Ah, I was hoping to see the other stuff." At my look, she said, "Joking, joking. Maps are cool." Embarrassment was seeping from her, so I tried to ignore the empath powers for a moment, at least in relation to these ladies. It seemed a bit of an invasion of their privacy... especially when it came to her professed interest in watching tentacle porn.

Erupa waved us on and held the door while we entered. It wasn't like last time, where we'd gone through what was probably a main entryway. Here it was darker, with mechanical debris lying around that looked like discarded parts from old trucks and ships. Here and there were boxes of explosives and strange vats of liquid, possibly leftover chemicals related to the hybrid creation process, I figured, and best left alone. The ceiling was about twenty feet up, made of metal like the rest of this place, but for some scattered barely-working lights.

"So he was just jerking off, right there?" Cheri asked.

"Yup, he had the screen propped up, one hand on his gun, the other yanking on his dick so hard I thought he was going to tear it off. He looked terrified, too, which was weird—maybe he was masturbating as a way of dealing with stress? I don't know, but either way he saw me, shot his wad, and tried to pull his gun on me just as he was cumming. Weirdest thing I've ever seen. Before he'd even finished, he was dead."

"What a way to go, though," Cheri said, shaking her head. She turned to me and said, "If you ever decide to kill me, make sure it's in the middle of an orgasm, deal?"

"I'm not going to kill you."

"But for argument's sake, if you were going to—"

"Wouldn't happen."

Letha chuckled, shaking her head. "You all are strange. No doubt about it."

"Thank you." Cheri beamed.

Since we were taking another route this time, we didn't see the glass cages or broad, open areas from before, but there were more of the rooms full of crates and strange areas that were probably testing facilities—judging by targets along the walls and patterns on the floors. At one room we stopped and checked the crates, finding spare robotic body parts and all manner of disassembled weapons.

Seeing as we were stocked up and didn't know how to assemble the weapons anyway, we kept on.

None of us spoke, instead maneuvering through this labyrinth under the planet so many knew to be their living hell. Down here the air conditioning kept the halls cool, fluorescent lighting on metal giving me the feeling of being a sardine someone was shining a light down on, and I wasn't sure if I was about to be eaten or crushed.

A few more turns and my empath powers were picking up something. At first I wasn't sure, but then it came across as the warmth of excitement, a sharp hunger for blood.

I held up a hand, focusing so that the lines of light appeared, then gestured for them to follow me as I moved on, cautiously checking around the next corner. A door halfway down the hall was ajar, a man walking away from us with an empty pot of coffee. Oh man, what I wouldn't do for some coffee right now. I sniffed, but the place only smelled of chlorine and... bubblegum?

A glance back showed Cheri leaning over me, and she grinned, then squeezed the smiley face on her tit—sure enough, it sprayed out a bit of perfume that smelled of bubblegum. Only, as I breathed it in my head felt clear, my senses alert.

"My little concoction," she whispered. "Forgot to use it earlier, but, since we're all starting to stink—"

I put a finger to her lips, shook my head, and

motioned to the room. After a moment, she nodded and held up four fingers.

"What's that?" I asked.

"How many I count in there," she said. "According to the voices. Or... Lilly."

My eyes went to the tiny teddy bear as if that would give me an answer, and then I turned back to the room. Even with my upgrade, it wasn't possible to tell how many there were. My best bet, then, was to assume she was correct.

Four. We could take four.

"I can take that one," Erupa said, gesturing to the man who was about to reach the end of the hall.

"Go," I said, gesturing, "but keep it quiet if possible."

The rest of us moved for the door, still slightly ajar, as she vanished, appearing again in front of the man and tearing into him. She even caught the coffee pot and gently set it aside before charging over to join us, where we were already pushing through the door.

"Dammit, Colderone, what'd you forget this time —" one of them started, only to freeze with his mouth open when he saw us. His hand went for an alarm while three others stood, drawing weapons.

But we had the element of surprise, and already had our weapons drawn with Cheri in the lead with her sword, me with my baton, and then Letha with a long knife. The hand went first, barely an inch from the alarm. Next Cheri sliced up and across the man's body as she turned to slide her sword into the next man's gut and up toward his heart. Letha kicked out a man's knee and then sliced his throat as he fell, while I blasted the last of them with a shitload of electricity.

The first, missing a hand and with a horrible gash on his front, was still alive, slipping in blood as he tried to move on his knees to reach the alarm with his other hand. I turned, ready to strike, but Letha beat me to it with a push kick that sent him falling back onto his buddy, followed by Cheri thrusting down and shoving her sword through his eye socket. *Game over, pal.*

Staring at these two now, I almost had to laugh at how much alike they were. Letha could almost be the older sister, Cheri the crazy younger one who'd never learned to give a shit about what the world expected of her.

They both stared at me with frowns, probably wondering what I was thinking, looking at them like that with a silly grin plastered across my face. Erupa was there, joining in, but was looking past us to a large screen behind me. There were several smaller ones around it, but this one read, "Main Feed."

On the screen, we could see an overhead view of the asylum, zoomed in to where a sniper was on the roof, taking out opponents who were trying to make a run on the main building at random and... I had to look closer to be sure, but someone was giving him head while he did it. These people were almost as bad as... well, me.

The shot changed to a lower one, giving a good view until it went wild and another shot showed a drone falling. Then it centered on a group at one of the guard houses, clearly planning their attack on the main building.

"How long can this go on before they realize Muerta isn't even there?" Letha said, pissed, but she was scanning the screens, very curious. Looking for something, or someone?

"Who is it?" I asked.

She glanced over, saw there was no point in denying it, and said, "I arrived here with two guys. A woman, too, but she was killed before we even got here."

"You came voluntarily?" Erupa asked.

"Not exactly, no. I mean, we meant to... This was the spot, they told us. If we wanted to hit Orion Corp., this right here was where to start. Only, the plan was flawed from the get-go, and someone betrayed us." She took a moment, looking over the screens again. "So… yes and no."

"But someone's still out there," I said, finishing the rest for her.

"I wish I knew," she said. "Two someones, actually. For all I know, they're dead… or down here."

"For their sake, might be better if they were dead," Cheri said, earning her a slap from Letha.

Cheri blinked, looked about to cry, then said, "Shit, sorry. Lilly tells me that wasn't very sensitive."

"What my often very kind and loving friend here is trying to say," I said, helping her out, "is that we hope we find them and that they aren't hurt in any way."

"We're missing someone too, is all," Cheri said.

"Right, the fairy girl," Letha replied, nodding. "I remember. And you'd rather she be dead than down here?"

"No, but… she's already so small, what could they do to her?"

Erupa scoffed. "Do you really not comprehend the perversity of some people's thoughts? I won't go into it, but let's just say we'd better find her fast if she is down here."

Cheri frowned, not liking the sound of this at all, and nodded. "In that case, agreed."

"Is there a way," I asked, selecting the newly-acquired maps from my wrist device and looking them over before turning back to the displays, "that we can switch to cameras down here?"

"Good fucking plan," Cheri said and took a seat where the supervisor had been minutes before, then started messing with the controls. It was less than a minute before she said, "Bingo," and then we were looking at all manner of monstrosities like we'd seen when we'd been down here before.

"I think I'm going to be sick," Letha said, as we started scanning the screens for any sign of Tink, or Letha's friends, all of us breathing heavily in anticipation, knowing this room could be the key.

13

Images of horrible sights continued to flash up on the screens, while some switched to views of Elites, who were now on the move. Letha took the door while we searched, but so far all we were seeing was how incredibly vast this place was.

"Son of a bitch," I said, leaning back and letting Erupa take over.

"Why do you care so much?" Cheri asked. "I mean, when you caught her, I remember the way you were taunting her when you brought her onto the ship. You were a dick. So... why?"

I thought about it, not sure at first. Then the answer hit me. "Because I was wrong. Wrong about so much, including both of you... and because you care. The way I see it, if you want to find her, she must be worth finding."

"That works," she said. "Though to be clear, I'm no superhero. I've done shit—maybe not enough to end up in the Abaddon Asylum, but don't mistake me for an angel."

"I—I really don't know what to do with that."

"Process it, accept that it's the case, and deal." Suddenly, she leaned over, looking excitedly at one of the screens, managing to almost put my eye out with her breast as she swung around. "Wait, there."

I turned, seeing what she meant on one of the smaller screens. It showed a room with several glass cages, and in one of them was definitely a small, winged person. From this screen it was hard to say for certain that it was Tink, but there was nothing saying it wasn't. How many fairies are out there, after all? The view showed them along with a round table and three guards playing a holo-game which involved cards that had monsters and warriors rise to attack each other.

"A breakroom," I muttered.

"They didn't know what to do with her, just that she was special," Cheri said, voice hushed with the realization. "This is good, right?"

"It's very good," I replied. "For one, because that means they might not have plans for her yet—though we'd better hurry. But also, because a room that size…" I pulled up my map via the display, projecting it onto the blank wall behind us, and manipulating it around like a square that you could enter. Most rooms were much bigger than this one, to allow for more display room, along with tunnels for spectators to walk past the displays as if looking at the exhibits at a zoo. There were several extremely large rooms, but not so many ones like this.

"Try sticking close to the surface," Erupa said. "If I'd designed this place, I'd have the breakroom there so I could get the guards back up topside if they're needed. Or near all those other things we saw, if there's a problem."

"Good thinking," I said, already moving the map as she'd suggested. Still nothing, as I maneuvered the map with my fingers, but then, just as I was starting to feel discouraged again, I stopped, finger covering what looked almost like a closet. I changed the angle slightly, though, and I could see that this room might be the right size.

"It's our best bet," Erupa said, eyeing it.

"Good," Letha said from the door. "Then let's move. We've got company."

"How many?"

"Not sure, but at least two. I ducked back in here before they could spot me."

I nodded, considering the best strategy. "They

might be checking on the other guards, and not have a clue we're here yet."

"Ambush," Erupa said, then ran her tongue along her teeth. "I like it."

We took the most intact bodies and put them back in the chairs, moving the others out of view, and then took hiding spots, waiting.

"Section Echo," we heard as the door swung open, "we need reports on—"

As soon as the first two had stepped in, Erupa did her thing and took out the one in back, still in the hallway, causing the speaker to turn at the suction sound of steel in flesh. He fell, a sword through his chest, a hand to his mouth. That left the middle guard who let out a grunt as he tried to pull his weapon, but I was on him with my baton to his windpipe, a good *thwack* that left him gasping for air before collapsing to the ground, dead.

"More could be here any minute," Letha said, assessing our work, a raised eyebrow showing she was impressed. "How long have you all been a team?"

I chuckled. "That's complicated."

"We have a destination?" Cheri asked.

At my confirmation, checking the map again and finding I could mark the room, we started off. These were the upper levels, but still the backside of this place. Orion Corp. clearly didn't have this set up to show off to their elite visitors. At first we were able to stick to the hallways, and here we saw stuff we wished we hadn't—thanks to Cheri peeking through a door she shouldn't have.

"Guys..." she said, and then gestured us over.

"We have to keep moving," Erupa protested.

But the look of fright in Cheri's eyes left little room for argument. We all moved back to the doorway, creaking it open more, and took turns cringing. I should've guessed by the smell, but that would've likely made me more curious. What we'd seen in there were tanks of body parts, some full, and there were tables with blood and more body parts. It was either where they discarded the pieces that they couldn't use, or else, their failed experiments. Either way, the fact that so many people were ending up like this made my gut turn— the smell of chemicals mixed with death didn't help either.

"Why'd you make me look in there?" I asked.

"In case there were any doubts about how jacked up this place is," she said, shaking her head, hands jittery as she spoke. "I'm taking these fuckers down."

"Or we'll die trying," Letha said, face pale at the sight, but strong.

From there we picked up the pace, only slowing

once when passing a side passage with several guards conferring over a screen up on the wall. They seemed to be discussing the movement of a tour group, and we decided it was best to keep moving, not draw attention to ourselves by attacking and risking any alarms.

There was more to the decision, though. As much as I was determined to take down Orion Corp., life still felt precious to me. Maybe it was a weakness, I don't know, but it held me back. I think it was my belief that everyone can change, that one minute someone can be hunting down the possible good guys, thinking they're bad, only to turn around and see the truth like a kick to the face.

If they tried to hurt me or mine, though, I'd have no problem tearing them apart.

We managed to sneak past, then rechecked the map, and were relieved to see we were close. Only problem, we had to pass through the viewing tank area to get to the other side, where the supposed breakroom with Tink was.

The door to the viewing area didn't present a problem, and soon we were out of the back halls, into an area that much more closely resembled the space where we'd first caught a glimpse of what was going on down here. It was a large hallway, with ceilings reaching three stories high with various displays along the way. At one point a man sat with no eyes, seeming to stare at us, and as we passed he burst into flames that looked like wings. Nothing out of the ordinary, for supers, but still creepy as hell. We passed displays with water and vampire mermaids like I'd encountered in the past, ones that looked sexy as hell one minute, pressing their bare breasts against the glass only to expose their sharp teeth and claws the next, as they scratched and slammed against the barrier trying to get at us. A man swam in one, completely nude and lacking any hair, and I wondered how he could swim so long without going up for breath, but as we passed his upper half transformed into that of a shark. Impressive, though when I noticed Cheri staring, it didn't seem to be at his shark head.

"Keep moving," I hissed, and she turned to me with a grin.

"Ah, do I sense jealousy?"

"Shut up."

She chuckled and the other ladies smiled, so I ignored them and kept walking. As if I wanted to be able to transform into a shark… well, yeah, that sounded kind of cool. But not at the price these people and supers were paying. There were so many, it was heartbreaking. Stuck in these glass cages, they had no life anymore—at least, not until Orion Corp.

decided it was time for them to serve a greater function, whether that be war, other forms of entertainment, or… I glanced back, considering the levels some elites would go to feel godlike, considering the mermaids—maybe food? The thought sent a chill down my spine.

There was no reason to believe that, I told myself. All of this was rubbing off on me, putting horrid thoughts into my mind. Several elevators lined the walls, but it wasn't until we had passed the fifth that one started to move.

"Someone's coming," Cheri hissed, stating the obvious.

Our destination wasn't far off now, but we didn't know how long the elevator would take, and the fact that it was glass meant we'd be easily spotted if we were out in the open. We turned, debating whether to attack or run, but Erupa was the one to speak up.

"If we attack the elites, this whole place will be on us in seconds," she said. "That'd be the end of us, but also a reason for Orion Corp. to rally, to declare open war against anyone it felt like. Let's not give them that chance."

It only took a brief moment of eye contact for us to all agree, and then we were sprinting for the door toward the end of the hall.

Almost there, I was certain we were actually

going to make it. That is until I heard Letha mutter a name—Darnell. When I turned, I saw her up against the glass, hands pressed to it, staring at a monster that only on second glance bore any resemblance to the man it might have once been.

The thing had green skin, darker green hair sprouting out of its body, and horns not only on its head but in places along the arms, including long ones from its elbows and knees.

"It's not him," I shouted, but she was already stepping back lifting her rifle before any of us could stop her, and firing into the top of the glass.

Shards of glass rained down around her and the creature, cutting both of them and making the thing howl so loud that, if the guards hadn't heard the gunshot or the breaking glass, they'd certainly find us now. The elevator cables were still moving, and it was actually possible it wouldn't even come to our floor, I supposed... but I knew that wasn't our luck.

"What've you done?" I asked, shaking my head, but turned to see Erupa staring with a mixture of confusion and revulsion. For the first time, I had a thought, and wondered if she was having it too— supers like her, with their horns and different colored skin... was there a chance they weren't mutated like that at all, but planted in society, genetically formed to look that way by this corporation?

Of course, from there the questions spiraled out of control. The implication could then be that any, or all, supers might be such genetically modified beings, myself included, but I refused to accept that. But doubts were taking over, so much so that my legs felt weak and I wanted to collapse right there until the room stopped spinning.

"We have to move!" Cheri shouted, gesturing for us to hurry. "Get your friend and—"

But this thing was no friend, as it clearly demonstrated when it charged out, slamming Letha aside with a powerful swipe of the arm that sent her flying into the far wall. She slid down the wall before falling to her hands and knees, gasping for air, while the beast turned on us.

"Don't…" Letha wheezed, holding a hand up. "Don't hurt… him."

"This isn't Darnell," I protested, cursing softly. "Not anymore."

She gave me a look, then turned back to the monster. "It's me, Letha. We met on Paradise Planet Fourteen, remember? Darnell, it's me…"

The monster growled, fueled by the pain of the glass, and turned on her with eyes full of confusion and anger.

"Your friend, Rand... is he here?" Letha continued. "Come, we'll find him. Together."

She held out a hand, as one might do to a pet, and it actually seemed to be working, but then the elevator slid to a halt.

"Shit," I said, stepping back, then looked over ourselves, trying to imagine how others might see us, and said, "Quick! Get to the door! If we have to, try to move like we're crazy, like we're escapees too." Better than them realizing that we had broken in. As I went, I slammed my baton into the glass of three more cages, freeing monsters with a burst of electricity.

An alarm sounded, and then we were pounding toward the door. I reached it first, then Erupa, who turned to wave Cheri and Letha in. Only, Letha was still with her monster, her Darnell. She was trying to coax it along when the elevator doors finally opened with a ping. The creature roared again, it almost sounded like, "Go," and then he charged the elevator.

Double shit. I stared in horror as the other monsters did the same, but to my relief, the guards in the elevator with their tour hit a safety switch, so that layers of metal shot up around for protection.

Letha hesitated, calling out to Darnell again, but then followed us, throwing herself through the door in a panic. I slammed it shut behind us, the sound of banging and more glass breaking echoing through the tunnel.

"It was him," Letha said, teary-eyed, unable to look at me. "I swear to God it was fucking him!"

I held out my hand to take her shoulder and comfort her, mouth open as I tried to work on what to say, when a voice said, "Letha?"

She perked up. "Rand. Rand?"

"They have me here," he said. "I'm... I don't know. It's a circular room, and—"

"Got it," I said, already pulling up the map as I'd recalled seeing only two circular rooms in the vicinity, and now that we were looking, only one made sense based on his voice being able to reach us. It wasn't so far out of the way, but the alarms were blaring.

"Meet us here," I said, indicating the breakroom. "Then we'll find a fallback point, together."

Letha nodded. "But I'm still going after Darnell somehow. He recognized me, he..."

"I know," I said, and we split paths, my two ladies and me charging toward the door at the end of this smaller hallway. It flew open, but to my relief only one guard was there now. It must've been long enough that the group we'd seen earlier had gone on its way, leaving only this one behind to guard the rear. He looked at me, then turned slowly to stare at Erupa, taking in her blue skin and horns.

"What's she doing out of her cage?"

That was all he needed to say to seal his death warrant. She tore through him with her shadow punch, her fist quite literally going through his chest. Death showed in his eyes and he collapsed, though no hole remained. She'd essentially burnt his heart to a crisp. It was both exhilarating and terrifying.

"Go," Erupa said, turning back to the other room.

"What?"

"Fuck the elites... I'm—"

A pounding sounded on the door, the three of us freezing, and then there was a familiar roar, followed by other strange animal sounds, variations on roars and hissing, and thuds.

"Le..." growl, "tha," I thought I heard, and clenched my jaw, thinking *fuck it* as I ran back, threw open the door, and stepped aside to let Darnell in. Somehow, Letha had been right. At least part of him was still there, if not completely.

On the other side of the door, the remaining monsters were tearing each other apart, having not been able to get through the metal to the elevator. On the far side, I saw doors opening and guards charging in. I quickly closed our door, hoping they didn't notice. I pointed, "Letha went that way." Darnell looked at me, seemed like he was about to attack, but then changed his mind and charged after her, each step thudding on the metal.

"Tink!" Cheri exclaimed. I turned and saw Cheri standing at an open door on the other side of the room. She'd found the breakroom. Erupa and I rushed over and there she was, at last.

14

Inside the room, Tink was in a smaller version of that same glass cell, glaring at us. We charged over, found a button this time that released her, and then motioned to her to get out of there.

"What the fuck?" she said. "I'm supposed to be relieved to see you all? We're best friends, at long last reunited?"

"No, but—" Cheri protested, motioning to the door.

"And you storm in with dickface here, this motherfucker," her wings were buzzing as she flew up into the air, hovering just out of reach as if I might try to attack her. "This shit-eating fartlicker, this—"

"We get it," I said. "But I'm here to help."

"Fuck you."

She flew for the door, only stopped by Erupa stepping into her path. "Trust him or not, this place is going apeshit right now, and we need to stick together to figure out an escape plan. Guards will be everywhere."

"I'm tiny. I can just fly through the ducts or some shit," Tink countered.

"And then?" I asked. "They plan on incinerating everything up there, practically. Starting over. You think they won't notice you if you do escape the flames? I tracked you down. I'm sure they'd find you, too."

Tink spun on me again, buzzing up close to my face, and pointed her finger at me. "You caught me because you got lucky! Because…" Her words trailed off as a large form filled the doorway. "What the shitstain is that?"

I turned to see Darnell there, Letha scooting past him with a limp man on her shoulder. He looked like he might normally be strong, a tall redhead, but at the moment he was simply defeated and confused.

"He's with us," Letha said. "We came all this way to rescue you, so are you done bitching and whining, and ready to get the hell out of here?"

Tink glanced my way again, spat, but then fluttered about, trying to assess the situation, finally settling her gaze back on Darnell. "Sure, fuck it. My chances might be better with you all, and worst-case scenario I take off whenever it's convenient."

Not even a 'thank you,' I thought as we headed for the door, but then Tink shouted and motioned for us to come back. She led us to a smaller door on the other side that none of us had noticed.

"Service passage," she said. "Saw some of the guards coming in through this way, and figured it's how I'd escape if I had a chance. Also where the toilets are, I gathered from their conversations... and I really need to take a piss."

"Are you serious right now?" Letha started, but Cheri cleared her throat, looking awfully worried.

"I wouldn't mind," I admitted.

"I've been holding it so long," Cheri said.

"Oh my..." Letha shook her head, then gestured for Darnell. "Can you fit in through there?"

He still had a monstrous look in his eyes but stomped past us without any trouble. He fit, but barely, and soon we were all through, in a much narrower tunnel with a ceiling only just a bit higher than Darnell.

"Actually," I thought aloud, "the service area... not a bad place to hide while all this is going on."

"And we need a place to clear his mind," Tink said. "The guards spoke about it... wondering how long it takes them to clear once they're out in the open—one said about thirty minutes."

"Clear?" Letha asked.

"Yeah, he's still in there, just drugged up from whatever gasses they put in those tanks. Probably similar to your other friend here." Tink buzzed over to Rand. "My guess, anyway, just based on what they were saying."

"As weird as it is to say this, then..." Erupa turned to me, and I nodded. "Right, quick bathroom break, all in one in case there's trouble."

Nobody argued, but we found only one bathroom anyway. It was large, at least—big enough for the guards, complete with lockers and an area for showers. Apparently, these people spent a lot of damn time down there, because they even had some food storages and water, which was a big relief for us.

Letha took the first watch, weapons ready with Darnell and Rand at her side. Erupa took the map device, studying the maps while I did my business in the restroom. I looked forward to a good break, and we figured that with Letha guarding the door and me countering the station's Quencher with my own, our powers would be able to warn us if an enemy attack came.

I had a moment to sit and think, going back to

that idea that Orion Corp., or even one of the other corporations, could have been genetically engineering certain types of supers all this time and inserting them into society. For what purpose though? As a test? To one day call upon them and activate some form of mind control to have them rise up? It was all speculation and all well above my pay-grade, or at least, it had been. From now on, I was going to get answers.

Before finishing, I pulled up my screen and was glad to see I'd reached level three. What was available wasn't drastic, but it looked like it gave me the ability to push emotions onto others, not just absorb them into me. I thought that there would likely be some interesting applications, but I wasn't sure what yet. Wait a second—I leaned in, looking at the second part of the description of my upgraded empath skills, and saw that it said "Healing applications." Monks back at the temple had claimed to be able to heal, though I'd never actually seen it. Could this be legit? Actual healing? I was looking forward to trying that one out, for sure.

Level three had given me another strength point, as well as endurance and defense, which I was grateful for. All of this was so reminiscent of what they'd taught me at the temple, though there it was attained through years of self-focus and training.

Here I was fighting to change the world, really making a difference. Maybe on some level it made sense, then, that these skills would come faster to me? I had to wonder if the being who'd made this equipment with her powers was some top-tier monk, or had at least some connection with the temple. Another question to find the answer to one day.

There had always been this one move in training that I saw others perform—a flying triple kick followed by a punch that they called the dragon's bite. Two kicks in the air I could do, but never understood the physics of the third. That was my problem, my *sifu* had always told me. "Don't try to understand, just do... but when you're ready."

Would I soon be ready? My enhanced speed and stamina might make it so, if nothing else.

Finishing up, I heard the sound of running water and walked back toward the showers, passing Tink who was at a sink full of water, her feet dangling in like it was a lake. She glared, but I could detect a hint of curiosity. At least she wasn't completely closed off to me being there.

There were several shower stalls along the wall, all curtained off, but when I entered Cheri peeked out from behind one, smiled, and then moved the curtain aside and went back to showering as if she hadn't noticed me. I stood there watching, blood flowing south as she lathered soap and ran it along her legs, up to her breasts and across her neck. She rinsed, and as the water sluiced the soap away, I watched it caress her skin, wishing it was my hands.

Everything radiating from her spoke of horniness and desire, but I was still too shaken by our recent events to be fully where she was.

"How do you do it?" I asked.

She gave me a pout, and said, "Really? That didn't do it?" A glance down showed she saw the bulge in my pants, so she added, "Or it did, but… what's the problem?"

"Physically, yeah, but mentally…"

"Excitement, the risk of death." She shrugged, turning to let the water finish rinsing her. "It doesn't turn us all on like it does me. But didn't you say you can absorb my emotions? So, absorb away."

I took a breath and then gave it a try. The change was instant and drastic. Where I'd been focused on blood, death, and near escapes one minute, now my heart was pounding with a new excitement for life, my cock throbbing as it threatened to break free of my pants.

"Now strip," she said, and I didn't need to be told twice.

When I had cast my gear and clothes to the

side, she gestured me in and began to caress me, lather me with soap, and then clean every last inch of me. Her hands found my cock and mine were running along her ass as I leaned in and pressed my lips to hers. With her level of excitement matched, the kiss was like that of two horny teens who can't wait to tear each other's clothes off and find out what lay beneath. But we were already nude, already finding out, and my hands couldn't stop exploring her, couldn't stop appreciating the curve of her breast or playfully pinching her perky nipples.

"Come on," she said when I was clean, and she pulled me out of there, grabbing two towels off the wall, and leading me to another door I hadn't noticed. It was a gym, complete with a matted floor.

She laid the towels out, and we sat down on them. We just sat there looking at each other, simply grinning, and then slowly we began caressing each other's bodies. My fingers entered her, her back arched, and then she moved in, kissing my neck and chest, lowering me so that we were both lying down, side by side with my leg over hers. My fingers moved gently, loving the feel of her soft, wet flesh, and she was moving her hand along my balls, kissing me passionately.

After a moment, though, she moved to my cock,

slowly stroking it, and I realized that this was more than pure horniness, more than borrowed emotions.

"What's happening here?" I asked.

She let her nose touch mine, giggled, and said, "Life."

As simple as that answer was, it had a profound impact on me at that moment, so that I held her close to feel her at my side, just to know she was real. Her smile was enough for me to know she was enjoying it.

"Did you know your parents?" I asked.

"A weird question at a time like this."

"Just... thinking, is all."

Cheri considered the question, then shook her head. "Not at all. You?"

"Me neither." I laid back, not wanting her to see me when I said, "It's weird sometimes, thinking that there are kids out there who grow up with normal families, who—"

"Wait, what?" she frowned, seemingly totally lost.

"I mean, do you think it's part of why you're like... this?"

She arched an eyebrow. "What? A Psychobitch?"

"Yeah."

"Right, um... no." She bit her lip to stifle a laugh, then let it out. "Sorry, sorry. But, when you asked if I knew my parents, I meant that I didn't *know* them, you know? Like they were mysteries, always keeping stuff from me, always trying to find ways of hiding their thoughts from my powers—and even when I knew exactly what they were thinking, it seemed to drive us further apart. Oh, they were around and even loved the hell out of me. I'm talking big parties, doll houses, reading me bedtime stories and tucking me into bed with a kiss at night. But to this day, I'm still pretty sure I don't *know* them, and never did."

"Oh," was all I could think of to say. Then added, "Wait, so you can read minds?"

"No. Not exactly... but my voices sometimes choose to tell me what others are thinking."

"I..." I wasn't sure how that was any different but shrugged.

"After all this is done," she said, "maybe we go find them, and you can help me get to know them!" She sat up, excited by the thought. "What'd ya say?"

"I—I guess I would like that."

She grinned, then laid back down, cuddling up and totally missing the point of what I had been going for there. Oh well, at least it felt nice to have her snuggling up against me.

"That's actually the reason for the name change," she whispered after a moment.

"From Lechas?"

"Yeah... It just didn't fit anymore. And my dad,

he'd always called me Cheri, old roots from Earth, he'd say, though I always wondered if he'd just found a book somewhere and picked it up. *Mon cheri*, he would call me when he was especially proud. I know I've messed up, life got away from me and all... but I'd like to think he's still proud of me. Somehow."

"With everything you're doing now?" I pulled her tight and kissed the top of her blue head. "I have no doubts."

Emotions of affection flooded over to me, and I lay there, opening myself up to the tingling sensation as it spread through my body. It was rare, this sensation, and I loved it.

A shuffling sounded and I looked up to see Erupa standing in the doorway, watching us curiously, a towel wrapped around her damp body.

"What, no show this time?" she whispered, though her eyes were moving over our nude bodies, hesitating at my still-hard cock. "You all are crazy, you know that?"

"Psycho, not crazy," Cheri said, then shrugged. "And hey, better than focusing on the negative, right? Nothing like a good dick to get your mind off of all the shit in the world."

Erupa frowned, pursed her lips, and then laughed. "Fuck it."

"As in... you'd like to?" Cheri asked, holding out

my dick for her as if in an offering. Erupa hesitated but Cheri added, "Don't be shy."

"I'm… trying not to be," Erupa admitted, and she slowly undid the towel, revealing a stunning body with voluptuous breasts. But still she stood there, uncertain.

"The voices tell me," Cheri said, turning to me, fingers tracing my shaft in a gentle caress, "that you have new powers, Ezra? That you can help her."

I gulped, feeling a shiver of pleasure run through me, and turned to Erupa. "Would you like that? For me to… help with your inhibitions?"

Erupa blinked, confused and uncertain, but then gave me a quick nod. It was the first time, but I focused on this peace and emotional arousal that had come over me and then imagined it flowing like a river rushing out from me to her, and watched as her posture straightened, her tongue running along her lips, and her eyes took on that hungry arousal I was so used to seeing in Cheri.

"This is… wow," Erupa said, and she walked over to us, kneeling at my side, and looked from me to Cheri. "Is this okay?"

Cheri took my dick and moved it back and forth as if unsure, but then giggled and thrust it toward Erupa. "Give it a kiss."

"A… kiss?" Erupa didn't look surprised though,

more excited. She lowered herself until she was lying on my other side, her hand running up my inner thigh until it nearly met my balls but instead moved around and came up to rest on Cheri's, still on my cock, and then she leaned in and gave the tip of my dick a gentle kiss. At first. The next came with more lip, saliva clinging as she moved away and then her tongue was running across it, and together they were stroking. I lay back, unable to believe this was happening.

"Ride him," Cheri said, pulling her hand away. She started to back up as Erupa moved up, her eyes flickering red as she straddled me and sent a warmth through her hand to me—a scary moment, as I knew what she could do with that hand, but it only added to the intensity.

When she slid onto me, it was the tightest I'd ever felt. It was almost painful, and I could see the same in her eyes, but then it was in and she was moving up and down, rotating her hips, and I was caressing her smooth skin, running my hands along her tight abs and up to feel her full breasts.

I glanced over and saw Cheri there, grinning. "Your voices tell you what I want?"

She didn't hesitate, taking my hand as I guided her so that she was sitting on my face and I was eating her out while Erupa continued to ride me.

Restrained moans came from both now. I was loving Cheri's pussy, slurping it up when Erupa's body started shaking so that she had to lean against Cheri for support, eyes closed and mouth open, holding back her final moan as she reached her climax.

It only took Cheri a few seconds to follow suit, apparently turned on by this, and then they were both there, off of me but having me stand as they knelt and worked my shaft at the same time— although Erupa had to be careful to keep her head tilted back, what with the horns, as Cheri had to remind her twice.

Every ounce of me felt like it was going to explode. My legs were shaking, even my abs, and then I felt so certain I was cumming—everything felt so perfect, but it didn't happen. They both looked up at me with confusion, but I was still rock-hard, still ready for more.

"Damn," I said, recognizing this feeling.

Erupa looked up in confusion, hand still on my cock, while Cheri stood and started kissing my neck.

"It doesn't have to happen right now," Cheri said. "Means you'll have more for later."

"I don't get it," Erupa said. "Did it happen, or...?"

"See, it's... I don't know how to explain it," I said. "It's only happened to me once before, and basically, right now I could go on for hours probably. Problem being, we don't have hours."

"We don't," Erupa said, finally getting it, looking a bit let down. "I actually noticed something in the maps…" Her eyes went to my cock and she stopped mid-stroke, wondering if she was supposed to finish now or what.

I cringed at the words, really wanting to spend the next two hours going at it with these two, but knowing that we needed to get back to the real action. With a breath and shiver running through me, I said, "It's okay. Rain check."

"I owe you one," she said with a grin, and then was up, acting really excited with all her previous weakness gone, and said, "Come on. The map."

We followed her back to where she'd left the gear, not even bothering to get dressed yet, and she handed it to me to run. When I pulled up the map, she indicated a spot down a few levels, toward the center. A room that had walls around it resembling a maze, and at its center… blacked out.

"The forbidden fruit," she said, finger on that spot. "Care for a taste?"

I loved that she had studied Earther lore, and though the reference was possibly confused here, I replied with a hearty, "Fuck yes."

On that note, I looked at us, all almost glowing. Wait, no—we were actually glowing.

"New upgrade," Cheri said, making her eyebrows dance enthusiastically. "A teammate bonus, adding buffers to those I'm close to. I guess you can't get much closer than we just did."

"No way," Erupa said, running her hand over her breast and then her purple nipple, watching the way the glowing light seemed to intensify at her touch. "I'm not sure what all this means for us, I mean... back there, that," she indicated my still rock-hard cock, "but I think we at least owe it to ourselves to have glow in the dark sex at some point."

"You're on," Cheri said, and glancing my way added, "and he's in."

Of course I was.

"Are you all..." Letha said as she entered, her voice trailing off as she saw us standing there naked, looking at the map and glowing somewhat, my erection in full view. "Ah, yeah... This brings back memories." She frowned, but then shrugged. "Do what you gotta do. Good news—I think they're ready."

"And it's been enough time," I said. "The guards are probably off searching for runaways or getting chewed out. Either way, it's probably a good time to move out."

"Maybe put that thing away first?" Letha said, indicating my dick. "Or… take care of it?"

"We will," Cheri said, then leaned in and whispered into my ear, "I hope my buffer stops you from getting blue balls."

I groaned. "Me too."

We quickly dressed and then Letha and Tink guided Darnell and Rand back to the gym, where we figured it was a better staging ground. Darnell and Rand were both looking very much alert now, though still beaten down. They'd been through a lot, after all. And as Erupa started explaining the plan, I had an idea.

I searched inside myself, trying to figure out how this healing function worked and then focused on simply making them feel better, trying to send whatever energy their way I could.

Everyone froze, turning my way, and I realized a low hum was coming from the back of my throat, waves of energy shimmering in the air between the two men and me, and a moment later they had clarity and energy in their eyes.

"What just happened?" Letha asked.

"Your friend here," Rand answered, looking at me with curiosity and appreciation, "he healed us. Or cleared our minds, anyway. Right?"

"I'm not sure exactly either, to be honest," I replied. "But some sort of healing, yes."

Letha let out a sigh and shook her head. "A world with supers. I'm not sure Earthers are ready for that. But thank you."

"Yes," Darnell added in a deep, growling voice. "Thank you."

The guy still intimidated me, so I replied with a simple nod and said, "Sorry for the interruption. Continue."

Erupa was about to, when Letha said, "Actually, it's a good plan but... We might have another part of it, one where we can add more value."

"Go on," I said, curious.

"The others," Darnell said. "Some are gone, true. Others... are like me. Salvageable."

Letha put a hand on his arm, a gentle touch that, surprisingly, didn't have any hesitation to it. "We're going back for them. We'll free them, get as many as we can out of here, up to the surface, while you take out the core. We'll have an army waiting for them."

"And if they don't send the ships?" Erupa asked. "If in all this chaos, they change their minds?"

"That's where you come in," Letha replied. "Taking out the core. If you succeed, they have elites on planet—employees, too, though I wonder if they care much about saving the latter. There will be a mad dash to escape this place, and we'll be ready to intercept it."

"If we all live," Cheri said, smiling wide. "Sounds like fun!"

"Indeed."

"Well then," I said, stowing the map and moving my hips to try to better hide the fact that erection *still* hadn't gone away and was tucked up into my belt at the moment. Hopefully none of them noticed, because I wanted to sound badass when those next words came. "Let's go blow ourselves up a planet."

15

We charged through the tunnel, knowing full well the chaos we were about to lay down on this planet. The idea that I could spare lives was more of a joke at this point. A plan of this magnitude had no room for pause, not when the result would likely be death for almost all left on the planet when we were done. Whether that meant us or not, we would soon find out.

All while Letha and her army of monsters caused havoc in the opposite direction, distracting the guards and making this possible. I hoped.

Tink fluttered next to Cheri, the two chatting in hushed tones as we went. Erupa was ready to use her shadow attack, I was looking at the map and focusing on my empath powers to search out guards before we might see them.

By this point I'd come to know the difference between the guards' emotions and the likes of Darnell. The latter came across as terrified or full of anger, and that's all I was getting at the moment. A quick check through a side door confirmed that Letha had her work cut out for her. More stacks of those display cages stood one on top of the other, going down several stories with walkways across, accessible by glass elevators.

Had I known anything like this was going on I would've walked away years ago. Instead, I was doing my part now, and had to hope Letha could save as many as possible. Regardless, ending this place was the only way to ensure future generations of victims didn't meet their fate here.

I had just closed the door and checked the map, seeing that we needed to veer left and then take a service elevator down three floors, when Tink suddenly charged me, transforming to regular size as she tackled me to the floor and slammed my head against the metal.

"You fuck!" she said. "You didn't even tell me we could use powers, you—"

I pushed calm into her with my upgraded

empathy power, and she fell back, confused, then looked up at me with even more rage than before.

"Tink," I said, sitting and backing away. "We're all on the same side here."

"You stay the fuck out of my head," she growled, and before she could lunge again I had the Quencher set to Mode 1 so that nobody's powers worked. Whatever she'd had in mind, she simply thrust her hand out at me and glared, annoyed that it wasn't working.

"Stop this," Cheri said, grabbing the woman and spinning her around. "He's not that man, not anymore."

"How do you know? Because you slept with him? The feeling of his cock inside you tells you he's suddenly not a scumbag, not the son of a bitch who—"

"No," Erupa interrupted, getting in Tink's face now. "That's not how it is. He didn't know."

"And right now," I said, pushing myself up and holding out my hands to show I wasn't looking for a fight, "we have a chance to make a difference. I thought you understood that."

Tink was still pissed, chest rising and falling with quick breaths. In her regular form, I was reminded that she was one of us, and guilt washed over me for how I'd treated her.

"You know he's right," Cheri said. "Even I know it… the voices tell me so, too."

"I'm sorry," I said. "I really am, but right now we have to get down there, deal with this, and then find a way to get off this planet. While I've done shitty things in the past, right now I'm willing to lay my life down to make amends, to make a difference. Can you at least give me a pass until it's all over, then, if I'm somehow still alive, give me this ass kicking I'm sure we all agree I deserve?"

My little speech seemed to be working, because her frown was fading. A look of skepticism remained, but she nodded.

"Don't expect me to smile and call you pal," she said with a sneer.

"I can accept that," I replied, then gestured down the hall.

She nodded, and then frowned. "I'd like to be small."

"You prefer that?"

"It's easier, honestly."

I turned the Quencher back to Mode 2, cancelling out the system's machine in our vicinity, and she reduced her size again, fluttering along next to Cheri.

"I didn't realize," Cheri tried to apologize, probably about letting her know our powers worked. It hadn't been her fault the fairy tried to attack me, though, so I waved it off. "We're all a happy team, though?" Cheri went on. "I mean, we're going to at least stand side by side as we kill all the bad people?"

"We are," I replied.

"Yup," Tink said.

"Well goody, Lilly was starting to wonder." Cheri held up her sword and smiled, striking a pose next to the bear, as if someone were taking her picture.

Rumbling sounded and then panels in the ceiling opened. Startled, we ducked into a room to our left, and watched as small flying robots went zooming past, all going in the direction we'd just come from. I had to guess the chaos had begun. Although, it turned out we didn't have to wonder long—suddenly we could hear a voice over speakers calling for all guards to respond immediately to a series of breakouts, and we turned to see a woman at her desk, staring at us with a mug raised to her lips, coffee dribbling down her chin and onto her nice, baby-blue suit.

All my thoughts about not hesitating to take a life got to me, seeing her, this woman who looked like any normal employee. Her hand moved for the phone, the other one dropping the coffee mug so that it smashed and she yelped—and then Erupa strolled forward, smashed the phone aside, and passed her smoking hand through the woman's chest. When she turned back to us, the woman lay slumped over, eyes hollow.

Erupa turned the monitor so that we could see the images of monsters and broken cages, while in other rooms guards were urgently shepherding groups of elite tourists, dressed in their gold and white clothes, to safety. It was definitely happening.

The rest was on us.

"Let me try this," I said, and took the wrist device with its maps, scanning the system and then playing with it for a second while Tink growled that we needed to hurry, but then I got it. Turning and showing them the holo display, I revealed that I'd been able to connect the link to the system, so that we could check in on Letha as we went.

"Well, fuck," Tink said, impressed, but then motioned to the door. "Still, gotta hurry."

"Not yet," Cheri said, and we all turned to see she'd found a water filter, and was just finishing up filling the pouches we'd taken from my wrecked ship earlier. "Would hate for us to die of dehydration, considering all the other options available," she said, turning to hold up the pouches and divvy out the contents.

"Okay, now we can go," I told Tink. She just

narrowed her eyes then turned, leading the way out of there.

Without another word, we tore after her and made for the service elevator, then watched on the map as it descended into the depths of Abaddon. We emerged into a hall of glass sides and bright lights— too bright, in fact, for us to see clearly at first. The elevator doors shut behind us and we ran out, but slowed to a walk as we started to realize what was on the other side of that glass.

The glass, I soon realized, was a series of one-way mirrors. These people were ignorant of the chaos above, elites with their robes around their ankles getting blowjobs from robots, others in private rooms with exotic supers with horns or bushy tails and animal ears, and in one, a man skull-fucking a mermaid.

It was all so disturbing, especially the way they would leer at themselves in those mirrors, watching their debauchery.

"Some people are fucccked up," Cheri said, shaking her head.

"When you think something's jacked, you know it's beyond normal levels of fucked up," Erupa said, and Tink actually chuckled, though it was clearly more of a nervous reaction than anything else.

"Do we stop this?" Tink asked. "I mean, is there a way?"

"There is," I said. "It's exactly what we're doing by going after the station core."

Tink looked at me, taking that in, and then nodded, fluttering along. None of us could be done with that place fast enough, hating the sights as much as the fact that this area was here. What did it mean, exactly? That Orion Corp. owners or employees would come here and watch the elites and all of this? Was it for monitoring, for research? Tests? If anything happened to the elites, there would surely be hell to pay, I thought.

But then, unexpectedly there was blood splashing, filling the mermaid's tank. The man in there with her was screaming, unable to get out, and nobody was doing anything to help him. Perhaps they were all off dealing with Letha's distraction, or perhaps this was something beyond my comprehension.

Either way, we exited that area and found what we'd been looking for—Engineering. Entering through double doors at the back of this hallway, we found the clattering noises of moving parts and all manner of electronics that didn't make much sense to us. What we were here for was the girder system that would allow us to reach the next floor down.

It wasn't easy going, but we had our powers about us and Tink scouting ahead, warning us about areas where viewing ports might expose us if we were seen climbing past.

"It just hit me," Cheri said as we climbed. "I can basically blame you for the fact that I'm not a mermaid right now."

"What?" I replied, annoyed that she was interrupting my focus.

"If you hadn't interfered, for all I know they might've made me into a mermaid by now. How cool would that be? Oooh, or maybe they do requests, like… give me a horn, right? Make me a sort of unicorn."

"Cheri, you do remember everything we've seen?" Erupa asked, concerned.

"Sure, sure, but I would be a badass mermaid, you have to admit."

"I prefer you as you are," I said, lowering myself to the next level, finally glad to be done with it.

"Awww, that's so sweet," Cheri said, then jumped the rest of the way and landed with a thud, still smiling.

I helped Erupa the last bit, earning me a smile for my chivalry, and then we worked our way past the beams and over to a new set of doors. Glancing through, it appeared dark within, but large. One of the huge rectangular rooms we'd seen on the map, if I'd followed it correctly.

"Beyond here, we enter the maze," I said, referring to the section of the map that looked overly complicated. "Stay alert."

"Thanks for the reminder, Mom," Cheri said with a scoff, pushing through the doors. She turned back to us and said, "Need a light?"

With a wave of her hand, we felt energized again and the glow returned, to all but Tink. Apparently, she wasn't 'close' enough yet. But the second we started to glow, a cheer sounded.

"It's time, ladies and gentlemen," a loud voice called out, and we were spinning around, trying to figure out what was going on. "Witness the amazing hunting powers of your new front line. Watch as these Champions of Abaddon are torn apart by your new army of Weres."

"Oh, shit," I said.

"Is he saying what I think he's saying?" Tink said, fluttering around my ear like an annoying fly.

"If by that you mean... they somehow think we're the prey for some hybrid Were-creature genetic modifications, to demonstrate how easy it is to kill even us, then yes, I think so."

"Keep quiet and turn off your lights," a voice said,

and I sensed emotion—confusion, anger. A bit of...
insanity, judging by the fluctuations.

"Cheri?" I said. "Can you...?"

"Oh, right." She waved her hand and the glow
vanished, but then a new glow appeared. Red
glowing eyes— three pairs— moving toward us.

The stranger—likely one of the actual Abaddon
champions who'd been brought down for this
demonstration—cursed and took off running. One
of the beasts charged past, a wind blowing by as if it
was the wind, and I sensed pure hatred and hunger.
These things weren't going to be stopped. Our only
hope was to end them.

16

Two pairs of red, glowing eyes remained fixed on us. They weren't exactly animals, because my empath powers didn't work on animals. Hybrids then, which made sense. And they were fierce, hungry, ready to kill—I got whiffs of all of that, though multiple people in the surrounding dark, enemies, threw my game off and I wasn't able to make any light to show where these others were. I just knew there were more.

"I count three of those things," Cheri said at my side, "and maybe three others."

"How?" I asked.

"Voices, of course." She reached over and gave my crotch a quick rub, then laughed. "For good luck!" She said, and then charged out into the darkness.

"She's fucking weird," Tink said, but then was charging after her.

"No use waiting for them to come to us, I guess," Erupa said, and gestured for me to lead the way.

I wasn't sure what I was feeling right then, but wasn't about to be the only one standing back while the ladies ran ahead. Giving her a nod, I took my arc baton in one hand and a pistol in the other, veering left to cover more ground and attack angles. A glance back showed Erupa doing the same, but to the right, her eyes already starting to glow in a way that matched the hybrid enemies.

I heard fighting ahead and to my right and was veering about when I pulled a signal from my left. Turning and sparking up my arc rod to see, I came face-to-face with a gnarly looking man, short but stocky and covered in tattoos, brands, and all manner of piercings. He was leaping into the air, a sword in his hands that sparked to life with electricity all over it as he brought it down.

No way in hell was I going to survive that strike, so I lunged sideways into a roll and came up, shooting. The shot wasn't great in the dark with only the light from our weapons to guide us, but it tore through one of his ears as he turned to face me. Blood dripping down the side of his face, he took a step and swung horizontal this time, but I leaned back, shot out his knee cap, and then lunged for my attack—electricity to the face, motherfucker.

That did the job, but then a beast that resembled a cross between a bear and a tiger came at me, tackling me to the ground with claws that scraped across my vest and teeth that threatened to tear off my face.

I unloaded my pistol into it, very aware that I only had two or three more reloads before running out, and even slammed my arc rod into its side on full blast. It still kept coming, all of this only angering it.

Tink appeared at its ear, thrusting her hands out so that waves of red energy flowed out and into his eyes.

She pulled back and said, "When he lets up, run!"

Her power, that I'd been very glad never to have turned on me, was one that caused someone to go mad temporarily. But from what I'd read, it was worse than that. Basically, the victim had to fight it, during the process essentially losing control of their body and, at the end, either beating it and suffering from a few moments of confusion and weakness, or falling dead.

It all depended on the strength of one's mind

before being hit. As strong as these beasts were physically, I doubted their minds could hold up.

As soon as the thrashing about began I was gone, rolling and pushing up. I caught a claw on the back of my leg that likely drew blood, going numb instantly but not impeding my ability to move. Then I was clear, some unlucky bastard who'd been sneaking up on me catching the brunt of the attack.

"Over here," Tink said and guided me toward where the others had taken down another of the beasts and now found shelter in the darkness behind what seemed to be the broken-down hull of a spacecraft, apparently in the midst of being worked on. And then we saw more of this place, machinery and whatnot. My best bet was they'd somehow automated the ship-building process and had a way of getting them to the surface.

"Thanks," I said, kneeling with the rest, eyes starting to adjust enough to get a sense of where I was. I caught Tink glancing my way, and said, "You didn't have to help me."

"Whatever, go fuck yourself."

I laughed. "Wait, you did help me just now. You realize that, right?"

"It wasn't my idea," she countered.

Cheri nudged me in the side. "Shut up and leave it at 'thanks.'"

I pretended to zip my mouth, then listened, realizing the mad roaring had died off, leaving only the sucking breaths of someone dying.

"That's some scary power," I told Tink.

She turned away, ignoring me, and then said, "Incoming, check your six."

Cheri was already moving, sword out, and caught the beast as it charged, a good sword swipe taking out one of its legs. The howl almost made me feel sorry for the creature but then it still managed to turn my way, and I didn't feel quite so bad. Erupa rose to take on a man who came at us from the other direction, while I lifted my pistol to try hitting this beast between the eyes.

A grunt sounded from our left and I prepared for another attack, but instead a man appeared with what looked like a trident, spearing the side of the hybrid beast in the exact spot to take it down and then kicking at it so that it toppled. He looked up at us, a wild man with flowing hair wearing only a loincloth, and grinned.

"Fucking hot, man," he said, nodding to me and then looking at the ladies. "All spoken for?"

"Yes," Cheri answered him, standing defensively with her sword at the ready. "And you are?"

A choking sound came from behind and I spun around, remembering that Erupa was fighting someone, but she emerged from the darkness cleaning a blade.

"We made a friend," Tink said.

"Trunk," the guy introduced himself, then said, "The wardens come next, I hear. We won't survive them. Not unless you follow me."

"And how can you help?"

Lights were turning on, highlighting new contenders as they floated in near the ceiling, riding spinning discs and carrying a variety of large blades and flashy rifles.

"I don't think it matters," Erupa noted, and gave the man a nod.

He looked my way first, and when I, too, gave a nod, he started running with us following close behind him.

"I've been planning this for some time. Had a few friends setting this up," he noted, "preparing for my time. Then word came that Letha had started an uprising down here, and—"

"You know Letha?" I asked.

He grinned the way only someone who truly *knew* someone could. "You bet your ass I know her, buddy. Used to be one of her top guys."

"Ladies and gentlemen," the voice above announced. "It turns out this show is about to become a slaughter. Feel free to stay, but avert your eyes if you don't like clean and fast."

"Fuck that," Trunk said, and he reached a portion of the wall, using his trident to jam, and then hitting a switch so that it, too, lit up with a burst of energy. In that brief flash of light, and with how he was squatting, I saw where he got his name from—dude was hung like an elephant's trunk. Not that I was looking, but damn, something like that is hard to miss.

A clearing of a throat came from behind, but when I looked, all the women were looking away. Possibly to the enemy, or more likely to pretend they hadn't been looking. Whatever, I knew who Erupa and Cheri were going home with, in a sense. Tink was a bit of a bitch—and not so much in a good way, though she was growing on me. Whatever she wanted to do was her business, even if that thing might be three times as large as her in her current state.

Trunk gave a heave as he stood, no longer revealed in all his glory, much to my relief, and the wall had an opening! He gestured us through first, as he turned and heaved the trident at the first of our attackers.

"After you," I shouted to Cheri, joining in to

shoot up at the enemy. A round of shots strafed our position, some bursting into flames, one bouncing off my shield. We were glowing, moving fast thanks to Cheri, and then the ladies were through and Trunk was shouting for me to go next, with him coming in right behind me.

He grunted as something hit him, so I turned and grabbed him under the shoulder, helping him along.

"Thanks," he muttered, and soon we were out of the main damage zone, turning left. The shots still came but didn't hit us.

"I can do one better," I said, and focused on my healing powers. Apparently my power didn't do physical stuff. The healing was only to the mind, at this level anyway, but he still seemed better for it and in spite of grunts of pain, was able to move on his own.

"There," he said, pointing to a crawl space and we went through, him before me as I set a mini-claymore in the path behind us, in case we were being pursued. These had been fun when on the hunt and outgunned, pinned down. An item that had a great element of surprise.

Turning back to follow the others, I wished I'd taken the lead, because in spite of the dark I still saw that damn trunk swinging back and forth as he crawled ahead. I focused on my hands, being careful to keep a good foot between us, and was relieved to see that the crawl wasn't very long. We were out of there and surrounded by a group of about a dozen other warriors like him, some in battle armor, some looking like cyborgs, and all glad to see him back.

"Letha's above," I said. "She found her friends, and they're creating an army of hybrids, fighting to the top. You should join them."

"You're not coming?" Trunk asked with a frown of confusion.

"We have business below."

Tink fluttered next to my head, glancing back and forth.

"Go, if you're not sure," I said. "If you don't know if you can trust me, still want to see me dead or my dick bitten off or whatever, I understand if you go. But we could certainly use you on the team."

"I'd prefer you stayed," Cheri admitted, then held up her bear. "So would Lilly."

Erupa gave a curt nod, nothing more.

"Fuck, fine," Tink said, and gave Trunk a mock salute, "May you slay many fuckers on your way!"

"Yeah, and maybe cover up that huge cock," Cheri said. "Lilly wanted to say that she found it very distracting."

He just laughed heartily and motioned to his friends to lead the way. "I hope you all kick ass, in whatever it is you need to do down there," he said, and then took off after them.

"Fuck, that was disgusting," Cheri said, shaking her head and then turning to me. "Which way?"

Erupa and Tink were both trying not to laugh, and I just ignored the comment, moving on. With a glance at the maps, I motioned toward the tunnel on the left, opposite where Trunk and his crew had disappeared, and we ran.

When we passed through the second tunnel we came out into another room like the large one where we'd met Trunk, though this one was empty. Charging through it, the screen above charged with light, whirring and filling the area above with mist.

"Hold!" a voice shouted from above, and there was a projection of a man in purple and gold robes, looking every bit the empress's loyal man. I knew this look, these types. I'd trained with them long and hard at the temple, studying their ways and trying to become one of them. How foolish, I now realized. "Ezra Faldron, our top hunter," the man on the screen said. "Just what the fuck do you think you're doing?"

I stood tall and shouted, "Taking you down."

He glared, then smiled... and finally laughed as

people streamed into the stands—those same viewers from the last room, I guessed? Did they not learn? And more. A line of attackers started forming behind us, in the direction we'd come from. Dammit, we were moving too slow.

"Taking me down?" the monk projection laughed. "How cute. How horribly, fucking, disgustingly... cute. You can't stand against me and you never will! Last chance, Ezra, and believe me, you don't deserve it. Lay down your arms, abandon this foolishness, and all will be forgiven."

"Is that so?" I drew my pistol, nice and slow, and said, "Here's my answer," then shot out the projection, before turning to reload and firing on the wardens.

Only half of his face visible now, the monk screamed out, "You will fucking drown in your own piss, do you hear me? Ezra fucking Faldron is no more!"

"Time to go," Erupa said, grabbing me by the back of my tactical vest and pulling, but the wardens were coming in too fast. I had to take some down. Breaking free, I pulled out two smart grenades that we'd taken from my ship, and threw them while kneeling and shooting the rest of my bullets into them even as the grenades went off.

People in the stands were shouting now,

trampling each other to get out of there. We were bringing out the full arsenal, but our escape route was blocked by more wardens, and supers who had apparently been called in for this.

The first super came at me with intense speed. There was only one option I could think of here, so I went in for the impossible—the dragon's claw triple kick. My confidence was soaring, my team at my side, fighting off more supers who moved at us faster than the wardens, and then I allowed our powers to go unfettered. Leaping, I got one kick to his thigh, the next to his midsection, and tried for the third. He blocked it, too fast for me, and followed up with a double punch to my stomach and chest that sent me onto my ass.

"Shit," Erupa called out as she used her shadow strike to come up on the other side of this guy and then take him down with claws to his throat, crushing his larynx with her strength. Apparently, her leveling up had done wonders for her strength.

She turned to help me up, another super landing at her back with an explosion of orange energy that sent her sprawling on top of me, and then I used what power I had when on my ass and unable to get up—throwing fear into the minds of those around me. It even showed in Erupa's eyes.

"Stay with me," I said, "you're stronger than them."

She nodded, and a moment later Tink appeared going full form as she dove out of the sky, knocking two back with kicks and then going small again to dodge their attacks.

"I found a way," she shouted, and appeared in front of me, pointing. "Go!"

It was the least guarded of the escape routes, so I had to agree. We were up and running, calling for Cheri along the way, and soon all of us were glowing again from her buffs, filled with courage and excitement by my borrowing from her and pushing into their emotions, and as we threw the last of our grenades and shot off numerous rounds into our pursuers, we escaped into the tunnel that would no doubt lead us more problems.

"This way," Erupa said, slamming into one of the walls as we went so that the metal bent and revealed a hole.

We didn't hesitate, going through and finding ourselves in the area between the walls, ducking under steel beams and only able to see by our glow, which was intensifying with each step.

At the far end we exited into a room where two creatures were already fighting each other, one seeming to be a man with pieces of him made from machinery, the other a hulking rhino of a man. We came in just as the latter tore off the arm of the cyborg and used the broken metal to slam into his opponent's throat, cutting through until the head was severed.

Men and women cheered, though the audience here was much smaller. One stood and shouted at us, calling for security, while the rhino hybrid turned on us, ready for the kill.

"Fuck me," Cheri said. "It's him."

It took me a second to realize they had literally taken Suari and turned him into a rhino. This was the first one I recognized as anyone that I had hunted and brought in, and that was a kick in the gut in itself. When he charged, the huge horn on his head weighing him down, I stood there in shock, wanting nothing more than to puke my guts out.

He charged me, but when I sidestepped and hit him with the arc baton, he didn't seem to care as he fell to the ground with a thud. He rolled and recovered, lumbering over and swung, but I caught him again. This time he tried plowing into me, and even knocked me over. There was no question that this man, staring at me with eyes full of hatred and self-loathing, was Suari/Rhino. But he wasn't the same as he'd once been, and now he wasn't attacking. He stood there, glaring down at me, eyes watering.

"Kill me," he muttered.

"It doesn't have to end this way," I replied, gun trembling in my hand.

"Please... do it." Tears formed in his eyes. "KILL ME!"

I pushed myself up and hesitated, but he came at me again and I had no choice. With that last shot, he stumbled back, then with my arc rod in his other eye he went flying, cracking the glass behind him so that whatever spectators were left stood, backing away in terror.

Rhino looked at me with blind, bloody eyes, smiled, and then fell limp. Dead.

It wasn't over though. Explosions and crashing metal told us the enemy was still in pursuit from the last room and we needed to get out of there. There was the control panel by the wall, but we wouldn't need it.

Tink flew through the air toward Rhino, at the last moment turning full size so that the momentum threw her with such force that she plowed into him, carrying him right through the glass. It shattered all around us, and we were charging up into the stands, tearing down guards in our path, and then out through the hall. We found another area that led beneath the stands and made our escape, to the outer edges of the walls and down, further and further into this planet, farther than the maps had shown, and now they were changing to show this. We were sliding along metal girders and areas that seemed like broken walls or incomplete in their construction. The walls had a distinct gleam and curving to the metal that I recognized often went with being created from the metal of meteorites, giving this whole place another level of intrigue for me.

We finally stumbled out into another level of darkness, breaking into a side tunnel, keeping on the move, always forward, always down.

As we stumbled through the darkness of yet another inner section of this horrible planet, I felt Cheri's comforting arm around me, her emotions flooding me with relief, telling me I'd done what was right.

"It's what he wanted," she said. "Plus, he was a fucking asshole. Seriously, tried drugging me once and I pretended to be out to see what he'd do... nasty fuck, I won't go into details, but yeah... he kinda deserved to die."

"You let him...?" Erupa asked.

"No. I mean, I stopped him before he got my clothes off, but he's the type who was so full of himself, talking about what he was going to do and all that. Bragging about past experiences. Honestly, don't feel bad. I wish you'd shot him in the crotch."

I frowned, unsure how to feel about that, and then tried to shrug it off. Best to move on from these situations instead of dwelling on moments that can't be changed.

17

We were in deep, according to my map. I wanted to keep pushing on, but finally Cheri pulled me around and said, "We need to rest, heal up. Check our location."

"Just do your buffer thing, or…" I started, but saw they were all exhausted, and she was shaking her head. "It's gone. The glow has been gone for a while, and I think I know why. Come on, we'll find a good hiding spot and I'll see about getting it going again. We'll need everything we have for this last bit."

I knew the truth of that, because I had recognized the monk. "I think I know that man," I admitted. "And if so, then yes, you're right. Come on."

From the map we saw that we were in the maze now but were able to find a room off of the beaten path. A likely dead end. Although, as we entered it I noticed the map seemed to change, and as I watched, it definitely did. Still processing that, I realized Erupa was asking about the man from the projection, the monk, and that she was waiting for an answer.

As we sat and dispensed energy bars and the last of our water, I told the story.

"When I was training at the temple, there was this legend, a man they called Master Shen," I started. "They said he has powers beyond our comprehension. A true Tier One super, but more than that. There are physical superpowers, and, according to the beliefs of all who followed the empress of those planets, mental superpowers that can be further trained and enhanced."

"Similar to our leveling up system?" Cheri asked, eyes wide and totally intrigued.

"Yes, as a matter of fact, though they don't present themselves in screens we can see. These levels require one of the masters to tell you when you've achieved them, as although some you can see in physical manifestations such as moving objects with your mind, others can only be sensed or felt by those with stronger powers. They said that only a true master can make such small manipulations of energy... in a sense, like the butterfly effect—a small change in the essence of our universe, major ramifications."

"Even Lilly lost you on that one," Cheri said. "But still, fascinating."

"My point is, Master Shen, this monk we're going up against, he was one of those who—I mean—I just don't know…"

"You're not sure you can take him on?" Tink guessed.

I nodded. "Back then he was this god to me, this legend that I strove to be like every day. Part of me still believed it could one day happen, until now, when I've realized it's not what I want to have happen."

"Which is?" Erupa asked.

"I want to be with you all. To make a difference. To change the system we have in place."

"And you will."

"To take this in… that all of it, even the legend I wanted to be so much alike for all those years, was a sham…" I sat in silence for a minute, then hit the ground with my fist before lowering my head. "Fucking Rhino… Whether he deserved to die or not, nobody deserves to be in this place."

Erupa put a hand on my leg, her head on my left shoulder. Cheri wrapped her arms around me from the right. We all let the silence go on, and then Tink fluttered down, landing on my shoulder.

It was a weird moment, my first contact with her, but all seemed forgotten when she leaned in and kissed me on the cheek. "You're a changed man, Ezra. I can appreciate that."

A hand moved to my right leg, then up it, and I glanced down to see it was Cheri.

"Is this really the time?" Tink asked, noticing it too.

"I was trying to find a good time to say so," Cheri replied, hand stopping while her finger traced a circle on my leg. "But I think the way my power gets charged, for my buffing of you all... is intimacy. Maybe not only sex but... it definitely speeds up the process."

"Oh, for fuck's sake," Tink fluttered into the air and moved away from us, turning to look at her. "Are you serious right now?"

Cheri grinned, hand continuing until it was moving along my crotch, starting to undo my pants. I sat there, totally wanting it—I still hadn't had my release from earlier, but almost agreeing with Tink that the timing felt off.

Almost, that is, until I felt Cheri's warm touch on my balls, moving them, cupping them and then going to my cock and pulling it out. Tink's eyes went wide and she quickly spun around. Meanwhile, Erupa was into it, helping to undress me, caressing my chest, taking my chin and guiding me into a passionate kiss. She placed my clothes on the ground and lowered me so that I was lying on them, and then started kissing my chest, her hand joining Cheri's to caress me below.

"Sure you don't want to get in on this, Tink?" Cheri said.

"I'm sure," Tink said, but then laughed.

"Don't be a prude."

"A prude?" Tink scoffed, turning to face us, and fluttered there, watching. We made eye contact briefly, and I couldn't tell because she was so small, but I was pretty sure she blushed. After a minute of them caressing me, stroking me, and Erupa running her tongue from the base of my balls to the tip, it was her turn to speak this time.

"Last chance, little fairy, or I'm going to finish him off."

Tink let out a heavy breath, revealing how turned on she was getting, though I sensed it anyway. She fluttered left, then right, then said, "I don't know.... Maybe we could settle a bet."

"A bet?" I asked, and then watched in surprise as she fluttered over, realizing then by the smile on her face what she meant. My hand went to my mouth to stifle a laugh. "You're serious right now?"

"Hell, I'm more impressed than I thought I'd be," she admitted. "Cheri, hold it straight up, would you?"

Cheri seemed totally lost, but intrigued. She took my cock and held it straight up, as directed. Tink landed on my pelvic bone, using Cheri's hand for balance, and then stood straight as she turned to face my cock.

"What'ya know," she said. "It's taller than me by a head. You win."

Both Cheri and Erupa burst into laughter at this, and then Cheri said, "What's his prize?"

"Prize?" Tink chuckled. "His prize is that he has a nice cock. Isn't that what all guys want?"

"Kiss it." Cheri leaned in closer, flicking the tip of my dick with her tongue before kissing it tenderly. "Just a little peck for his big pecker. Come on. Kiss it, kiss it, kiss it."

I felt my cheeks warming, but also my cock stiffening. The funny thing was, Cheri seemed to be even more into this than I was.

Erupa joined in the hushed chant. Tink finally turned to me, hands on her hips, and said, "You want this?"

"He's a guy, of course he does!" Cheri protested.

"What man wouldn't want a tiny fairy slobbering on his cock, worshiping this giant monstrosity like it's the largest thing she's ever seen?"

"Um, that's never exactly been one of my fantasies," I pointed out.

"So you don't want it?" Tink asked, wings flapping as she lifted off, but didn't go anywhere yet.

I hesitated, then whispered, "I would."

She considered me, then my cock, and fluttered back to it, landing on Cheri's pointer finger so that she could lean over, daintily, and press her lips to the smooth, red skin of my cock's head. It tickled, barely causing a sensation at all, but watching it was, as Cheri had said, fucking hot.

"You like girls with small hands," Tink said, running a finger along the curve of the point where shaft meets head, "I'm the girl for you."

She laughed, then fluttered off to land on the ledge above.

"Aw, done so soon?" Cheri asked. "I was just starting to get into that."

"It was sexy," Erupa admitted. "In a very twisted way."

"You try being my size when cum comes flying out of that thing," Tink replied. "Made that mistake once in my life, never again. Finish him off already."

Erupa leaned in, taking my balls in her hand, massaging them as she said, "With pleasure."

I was lost in bliss as Erupa took me in her mouth, distantly aware of Cheri reminding Tink that she could grow big and join in normally, but Tink replied by saying it wasn't time, that she wasn't ready yet.

The word "yet" stuck in my mind, and as if the fact that these two sexy ladies were on me wasn't enough, I was filled with an extra level of arousal of the prospect of Tink joining in, and all of them seeming very into the idea.

Erupa looked up at me with her red eyes, her hand glowing as she caressed my leg, sending sparks through me and making my back arch. My cock surged as she took it out of her mouth and flicked the bottom of its head with her tongue, then stroked it as she traced the base to my balls, licking and kissing and taking one at a time in her mouth.

Cheri watched, intrigued, and then undid her top and pressed her breasts against my face as she reached down and fingered herself. I was caressing her breasts, pressing them together against my face and then moving to take a nipple in my mouth, flicking it with my tongue before seeing how much of her breast I could get in my mouth at once. She was kissing my chest, moaning and fingering herself harder and faster, while Erupa stripped and then crawled teasingly up my body before sliding off to one side. The two helped me to my knees, hands sliding across my skin in heated caresses. Then Erupa bent over in front of me and had me take her from behind, pushing back as I slid in to the hilt, both of us moaning in pleasure. Cheri moved to stand above her, presenting her pussy, and I was eating it up as best I could while thrusting away, responding to Erupa's increasingly faster rhythm. Cheri pulled away, turning and placing her hands on the wall, and stuck out her ass. Erupa pulled off of me slowly, dragging out the pleasure, then stood and helped me up before guiding me forward and using my cock and her fingers to toy with Cheri's moist pussy. After teasing her until her legs started to twitch, Erupa guided me into the woman's other hole.

It was tight, and I winced, glancing over to see Tink there staring, fascinated. I had to laugh at how blatant she was about watching, not even trying to hide it this time. She grinned and said, "No way is that thing ever going near my asshole."

Cheri laughed but then said, "Shut up and slap my ass," so I did, a bit too hard I thought, and then thrust back and forth, my balls swinging and slapping against her legs and pussy.

Erupa reached under and cupped my balls, and then knelt and stuck out her tongue, so that I was lost in a moment of confusion and bliss. Her grip was firm on my balls, her tongue wet on my ass, and she was guiding me now, and then I was about to try and pull her up, to take her again, when Cheri pounded the wall and let out a long moan. I closed my eyes, moaning in return after seeing two blue fingers below me, fingering Cheri as I continued to fuck her in the ass.

I couldn't keep my eyes open and was nearly collapsing on Cheri's back, my hips pressed tight to her ass, my hands squeezing, and I released, cumming for what felt like forever and over and over.

I opened my eyes to see Tink there, still watching and now with wide eyes.

"That was hot," she said. "I'm not gonna lie. Damn... hot."

"You're telling me," Cheri said, and she pulled me close, not wanting me to exit yet, and then she motioned Erupa around. "Time for dessert."

I wasn't exactly sure what she meant, but then Erupa was there, looking unsure herself, but following Cheri's orders. Cheri reached back and put her hands on my hips, pressing down and cueing me to go with her as she sank to her hands and knees, my cock still in her ass, still mostly hard. Now *that* was a maneuver! Then she bent over and started eating out Erupa.

"I don't..." Erupa started, then her eyelids fluttered and she let out a moan. "Not with... women..." Another moan, and this time she let her head fall back, mouth open, saying, "By Oram, yes... yes... Fuck, yes."

And watching this, I was hard again, and started moving in and out, slowly at first, until as Erupa started orgasming, so did I. Again.

When it was finally over, I pulled out with a plop, fell backward on the floor, and just sat there for a moment.

"Damn, anyone have a wet wipe?" I asked, and they chuckled, Erupa still with her eyes shut, disbelief washing over her.

Cheri wiped her mouth, glanced over at me and said, "Use your underwear, then toss it."

"I..." It was gross, I had been about to say. That I couldn't do that. Then again, fuck this place and everyone who worked here, especially since we hoped to destroy it, possibly blow it up in the process.

So I did just that, first letting her catch whatever spilled out, and then folding my boxer briefs to get a clean section and using a small splash of water to get clean. If I died here, there was something weird about dying with cum and whatever else on my dick that didn't sit right with me.

For that, and now that the excitement of the passion was over, it was hard to look Tink in the eye. To distract myself I pulled up the map, showing it to the ladies.

"See, when we first arrived, it was like we were here," I said, indicating a section of the map a bit to the left. "Now, we're here."

"Like it's shifting, rotating," Erupa said, fastening her shirt and hiding those perfect, blue breasts. Too bad.

"Or maybe it's more than that," a voice said, and then the maze adjusted again, this time so that a wall of our room shifted with a grinding noise, and there was a hallway in front of us. I recognized that voice.

"Master Shen." I stood, checked my fly, and said, "What's the meaning of this?"

"You want me?" he said. "Now's your chance, you little piece of shit. Come and get me."

18

"Nobody talks to our man like that and gets away with it," Cheri said, sword held ready as she led the way.

Maybe charging right in after Master Shen like this wasn't the smartest move, but as far as I was concerned, it was necessary. We'd come for him, and we didn't have a lot of time. At first the halls were merely that, though I had to keep the map open to monitor when they would change and how. And just as we were letting our guard down, the gas started filtering in.

"Stay down," Tink said, growing large and flapping her wings, clearing a path.

"It won't be that simple," Master Shen said with a laugh. "But sure, keep trying."

He was right, because at the end of the tunnel a

wall appeared, another behind us so that we were trapped. I searched for him with my empathy power, trying to get a line, but he was too far out of range.

"Ideas here?" I said.

"Depends on how thick the walls are," Erupa replied, her eyes glowing, her hand smoking. As her hand turned bright orange, she placed it against the wall and pressed. At first the metal just grew hot, the room too, and I thought she might fry us. But it began to give way and a hole appeared. She pushed through, bending more, and then there was room, and we all climbed through.

"His dungeon won't do him any good if we can break through the walls like that," Cheri said, nudging Erupa. "Nice work. Ooh, idea!"

"We could use some," I said, noting how the room we now found ourselves in was starting to rotate and wondering what Master Shen had in store for us next.

She lowered her voice, in case he was listening, "Backtrack. One of those rooms was close, right? Where they're building ships and whatnot?"

I checked the map, and sure enough, we could reach one without too much trouble. He was defending the inner section of this maze but hadn't seemed to consider that we might go the other way.

Not sure it would work, I tried pushing out

aggressive emotions in case he was susceptible, trying to make him think we were about to push the attack, and then we turned and ran. It took a moment for him to react, but by the time he had the walls moving, we were busting through the next section. We charged on like this, having to take down two more walls and once needing Tink to go through and open a door from the inside, but then we were out of the maze and found the construction room.

"What's the plan?" Tink asked, fluttering about and then turning back in confusion.

I saw why the plan wasn't evident, as the spaceships they were building mostly seemed half-finished at best.

"Not those," Cheri said, indicating some machines for moving equipment. "There." One of the machines wasn't for equipment at all but seemed to be for mining work. "If the walls were indeed formed from the metal of local meteorites, they must have needed mining equipment if they did it locally."

"And we're going to... mine?"

"Essentially," Cheri said with a laugh, already jogging over to check out the machine.

"Sounds good to me," Erupa said, and then nodded at us encouragingly to come on, before running after Cheri.

"And if that doesn't work?"

I pointed to one of the half-finished craft. "Blow up a few of these, hope that'll be enough to take this place down."

"Hmm, I'll take option A."

Tink and I hurried over to join the other two ladies and found Cheri and Erupa working to attach a couple of guns we found onto the drilling machine. The thought worried me, as I had no idea if they knew what they were doing, but I moved inside and got familiar with the controls.

"All rigged up," Erupa finally said, and we were all in and I started the machine, feeling the excitement as it rumbled to life.

"Here goes everything," I said, and then we were rolling across the floor, picking up speed, and strapping ourselves in. "Hold the fuck on!"

As our first test, we went straight for the wall, mining equipment on and turning, massive drills and bits meant to cut at meteorites like teeth chewing through steak—okay, maybe I was getting damn hungry and craving a juicy piece of meat— but you get the idea. We hit the wall and, sure enough, were through in a matter of seconds, and then it was down through declines and all, Master Shen was shouting at us, warning that we'd destroyed our chances for escape, as he sent walls to crush us and shocks through to try and take us out.

But this mining machine was a beast, and no matter how much he threw our way, we kept going. We fell through a section to land almost perpendicular to the core, now tearing through what was basically the floor, and as soon as it was open, Erupa let rip with the remote-operated guns they'd mounted so that the next section down was already in tatters when we hit it.

Apparently, we were starting to get the heat off of Letha, too, because now wardens were appearing, striking at our hull and doing their best to damage us in any way possible.

"My turn," Cheri said. It turned out she'd affixed some weapons too, because now she pulled out detonators and started shooting them off, some in the back so that instead of driving forward we were propelled, slamming through walls and tearing our way to the center of this place. Then she launched one large missile out, and I had to wonder how the hell she'd managed that—but only for a split second before remembering that she too was a super—and seeing what was happening, started worrying for my life.

The missile hit and exploded, fire tearing back our way. We hit and tore through the wall there, but had swerved sideways now, losing all control, and the back of our vehicle had torn open, Tink hanging on for dear life.

Alarms sounded and warning lights flashed.

"Time to jump ship," I shouted, and when we came to a thudding stop, everyone unstrapped and ran for it, moving to our left, ducking into another tunnel as the vehicle too exploded, sending shrapnel into metal nearby in almost a musical moment.

But we were safe, for now, me pulling up the map and letting out a breath of relief. We were past the maze, almost into the inner core.

"The wardens?" Erupa asked, standing with hands behind her head to catch her breath.

"I have a feeling," I said and pulled up the feed of Letha. Sure enough, she was with a group much larger than we'd last seen, fighting the rest of the wardens who hadn't been recalled to deal with us. Bullets strafed their position, lines of fire going up. Some supers were certainly among the group, so I knew what we needed to do.

"Find the Abaddon Mega Quencher," I said. "The supra tech that's blocking their powers."

"You have a plan?" Erupa asked.

"You bet your perfect tits I do."

She frowned at my choice of words but then

smiled. "Let's get to it then, instead of sitting around complimenting my tits."

"Right."

We ran on, my best bet being that we'd find the Mega Quencher in a central, well-protected location. Likely the same location as the core, of which we were right outside. But if that were true, our enemy couldn't be so far away now.

I traced him based on his emotions of anger—hot, heavy—and found the line of his light, and then said, "Erupa, you're up."

She looked at me, then the path I was indicating, and frowned. With a deep breath, she nodded, then vanished into the darkness.

A scream followed, a thud, and all of us looked at each other in horror, wondering what we'd just sent her into. But then... the doors opened! We ran, charging, and dove in just as they started to shut again, Erupa shouting that she couldn't hold them.

And then we were in, she was there by herself and I was confused. Searching for emotions, I found him—Master Shen... afraid!

"He was here one minute, sensed you all coming," Erupa said, kneeling and looking like she'd just had the shit kicked out of her, "and then he vanished."

I went to her, doing what I could with my mental healing to give her energy, and noticed her glow as

Cheri did her thing, too. After a moment, she accepted my hand and stood, taking in our new surroundings with me. Master Shen wouldn't get far, but first we had to deal with this.

We'd made it. We were in the central hub. A large room with doors on six sides, walls covered with wires and cables and in strange metallic patterns. The center of the room had a glowing metal rectangular box the size of a human, but on the far side was the item that caught my attention. An amplifier that held the supra tech we were after—the largest Mega Quencher I'd ever seen. Unlike the small one that rested on my belt and looked like a fancy timepiece, this one was like a bookshelf of cables and motherboards, connected to one crystal in the middle where the superpower had been stored to make this possible.

With my first step into the room, the other five doors opened and wardens entered, armed to the teeth and ready to defend their precious supra tech.

"You've made it this far," Master Shen's voice came from the one opposite me, closest to the Quencher. Had he gone off to heal? Regroup? Regardless, the warden he was speaking through looked ready for a fight. "But you'll never leave this room alive."

Ignoring him, I sprinted for it and shouted, "Get me to the Mega Quencher!"

My ladies charged out taking the lead and attacking as they cleared a path. I ran between them, and when the way was open I lunged, taking my Quencher and opening it up, not sure what to expect. I had to get it to work as a counterpoint to the Mega Quencher, on a large scale, so opened up the latter as well and found a similar construct. All I had to do then, I realized, was attach mine to this beast, and use the switches. I hoped. As soon as I had it rigged, I gave it a go—only to have the crystal in mine explode. A moment later, though, the Mega Quencher's lights went bright and then popped, and the crystal burst in this one as well. It wasn't what I'd intended, but at least it wouldn't be blocking anyone's powers up above, as it was clearly destroyed for good.

And with it, we all felt a surge in powers—I knew because my empath ability showed them all as surprised as I felt when it hit. It was all we needed to put the final push in order, expelling the wardens and securing the immediate doors. A quick check on Letha showed that the wardens were having a hard time with her group now too, as supers started busting out all manner of crazy attacks on them.

While the wardens were powerful A.I. in their

own right, standing against an army of supers wasn't their best move for survival. I laughed at the sight of Letha looking heavenward and closing her eyes, as if thanking some other being for the help—funny, knowing it had been us.

But it wasn't time to watch them. It was time to turn our attention to the station's core. There it was, in the center of the room. A large, black box of metal with glowing lines that curved into signs like ancient runes. The top was a lid like a sarcophagus, and if I were letting my emotions get the better of me, it would've freaked me out. There wasn't time for that, so instead, I strode up and pushed. Nothing.

It took all of us together with Tink in regular form to finally get it to budge. Cracking open the core, we were shocked at what we found. There was a man—a super for sure, but not Master Shen. He was connected with cables and wires to this machine, curled up in a ball and half-submerged in slime. We pulled his slimy, nude body from the box, disconnected him from the wires, and laid him against the outside so that he was resting there.

He took a deep, shuddering breath and then his eyes sprang open. He stared at us, confused, hardly able to take it in.

"Who... are... you?"

"I'm Ezra Faldron," I told him. "And I've come to put an end to this."

He stared at me with defiance, his emotions unreadable. This told me he had to be a very powerful super indeed. Likely a Tier One. And then, suddenly, tears streamed down his cheeks while he still stared, and I realized he wasn't being defiant of me, but of some other force.

"Make it stop," he pleaded, and then thrust his arms out and floated up so that he was hovering above the ground, glowing blue. "Make it stop! End him, destroy Master Shen!" The blue glow intensified, the tears disappearing as his face took on an expression of pure victory and he said, "I will help you, in every way that I can."

And suddenly he exploded, but not in fire. Instead, he separated in slow motion like a fractured crystal, splintering, and flying out. Only, it was contained, and formed back into a swirling mass that regrouped and then shot out, tearing down the nearest wall and then all the walls after that, until all that was left was a gaping hole and, beyond it, the staggering form of Master Shen as a blue mist faded around him. The man had sacrificed himself so that Master Shen couldn't run anymore.

The bastard looked up and our eyes met. It was on.

19

I summoned all of my powers, pushing them toward that man, Master Shen, and then charged. Without anywhere to hide, anywhere further to run, he stood his ground, wrapping his monk robes around him and preparing for the fight to come.

And yet, he was every bit the master of legend. My strikes came hard and fast, but he was like a ghost, fading before them, moving about me and connecting hits. Erupa attempted her shadow attack, but he was prepared, kicking her with a back-kick that sent her flying, and left her gasping for breath.

Cheri came at him from the other side, her sword nearly hitting him, then pulling back as Tink sent her blasts of energy toward his mind, but he repelled both with a force that erupted from his hands, purple energy flowing outward like a shield. It hit a very surprised Cheri, and her sword went flying out of her hand.

She yelped, and I tried to strike while she reached out, her sword soaring back into her hand so that she could seamlessly keep her up attack, as we came at him from both sides. Then Erupa was back in there with her claws and a knife, but none of us could land our attacks.

He growled and thrust out at Cheri, striking her arm in a way that would have splintered anyone else's bones, but her power protected her and she merely stumbled away. His eyes went wide as Erupa's smoking fist came in and connected, singeing the shoulder of his robe but going no further.

I thought for a moment that we had him scared, so came in hard with an attack from my baton, but once again he blocked and then kicked me back, twirling with a scorpion tail kick to knock Tink out of the air when she went full size in one of her flying kicks. Next, he kneed Erupa in the chest and spun her over, striking her with his open palm so that she went sprawling. A final elbow to Cheri's temple and then a monkey paw to her stomach sent her back so that he had room to perform his next move.

Energy swelled around him as he spun, robes

trailing his limbs and becoming like a whirlwind, and then it was like the air around us became hard. The energy encircled the two of us so that when the ladies tried to fight it and re-enter the fray, they were blocked by an energy field. They pounded, using all the powers available to them, but nothing worked.

"I recognize your energy, boy," Master Shen said, now standing in one place, one hand above him, the other held at his abdomen, ready to call upon his powers. "But your *mana* is weak, your level nothing compared to me. Without your friends, how can you hope to be a challenge?"

"Fuck you, that's how," I said, and then charged.

First, I pulled both pistols and fired until there were no more bullets, but he merely swung his arms around, his cloak absorbing the shots and leaving him unharmed. Then I had my baton out in one hand, a knife in the other, and swung. He hit me with open hands, blocking and striking so that one hit to my sternum left me staggering back, out of breath and feeling like my heart would give out.

But I made up my mind that this wasn't going to be how I went out. I charged again, this time giving him the full blast of electricity from the arc baton, but he braced himself and absorbed it, so that when he came back with his strikes, each move released some of that electricity back upon me and the final blow left my head feeling fried, my weapons on the ground.

Having used all at my disposal, I stood and attempted the dragon's claw. It was all or nothing at this point, and time for me to take this fucker down. The first kick actually connected, but the second met his forearms and then he spun, slamming me to the floor.

All breath left me, darkness taking over, fading in and out—and my body arched, for a moment seeing my ladies there, calling for me, trying to break through to help. None of this was about me anymore, nor even only about them.

I was fighting this piece of shit to make up for all I'd done, to make the world a better place. Maybe I instinctively pulled energy from Master Shen, though he started blocking me as soon as he sensed it. Whatever it was that happened next, I was able to push myself up to block his ax kick and even push him back.

My breathing intensified, my mind refusing to give up, and I was back in there, performing the flaming arrow technique—a series of punches, kicks, and elbows I'd studied for many hours at the temple.

He grinned, then laughed as he blocked. "All you

know, I have mastered. Much of it is a technique I invented. You have no chance to stand against me."

Maybe not, but I wasn't going to give up. Not now, not ever. As we were fighting, my screen kept popping up with new items that I hadn't seen before. Defense times two, thirty seconds, attack times three, forty-five seconds, and more—and I glanced back at Cheri to see her focused and glowing. That's when I realized that I wasn't really alone and that even if they weren't inside this energy field with me physically, still they were at my side. My empath ability pulled in energy, mentally preparing me for more damage, physically telling my muscles to keep pushing on.

"How... are you... doing this?" Master Shen demanded as I pushed the attack, my strikes landing now more times than not. Even though he knew the techniques I was using, my attacks were getting through his guard.

"I'm never alone," I said. "Not anymore."

"Don't give me..." He took a hit to the chest, stumbling back, and glared. "...that shit. The world, all of this... it's you and your power, nothing else."

"You believe that, then you're a fucking idiot."

Again I pushed the attack, stat increases and buffers, even shields now forming around me. My muscles felt like they were growing as I struck, bursting in my clothes, even my dick started to harden.

"Oops, sorry about that one," Cheri shouted, and to my relief, the boner started to fade. The last thing I needed in this fight was distractions from my cock.

Tink laughed, and the sound of her laughter, like tiny bells, made me laugh, so that when I struck Master Shen again, it was with joy and vigor, and a harder strike than anything I'd managed to land yet. He spun away from the force, held out his hands and then moved them in great circles, preparing a defense, but I sidestepped, took his left arm before he could attack, and flipped him through the air so that I was able to hit him with a roundhouse kick and send him flying back.

He landed, staggered, and fell to one knee. Instantly he stepped back up, preparing to strike again, hands circling and calling upon his *qi*, but I wasn't about to let him have the satisfaction.

Pulling deep within, knowing he outpowered me in every way, I said forget the powers, forget my weapons and leveling up, it was time to become the man I had trained to be all those years ago. Only now, I was a better version. A version who knew the truth and fought for it. A version with people to care for, I reminded myself as I looked up and saw the ladies struggling to reach me, pausing at that moment and knowing I had this situation under control. They believed in me. *I* believed in me.

All of that flowed through my mind in a split second, clearing it and allowing me to see myself and this murderous son of a bitch clearly, to watch as if from the outside as I came at him with a left kick, still in the air with a right. Using the momentum of the strike as it connected with his midsection, my body spun and I caught him with a third kick, this time to the head. He started to fall—but not before I thrust my body forward and brought the tiger's claw in for the final strike.

My fist connected and it wasn't about superpowers—or maybe it was and just reached beyond my comprehension of the subject—but I felt at one with the universe and felt its power charging through me to explode into this man's body. The force threw him back so that he flipped and landed on his face, then kept ravaging him with waves of energy. His body twitched as his eyes rolled back, and yet... he was fighting it.

That son of a bitch was fighting it!

But the barrier was down and my ladies charged in, throwing everything they had at him, using their powers to attack. And then I knew that it only needed the final piece of the puzzle. I braced myself, expecting resistance, and attacked his mind with everything I had, boosted by Cheri's powers. In his weakened state he had no defense, so when my attack on his mind made contact, it was crippling.

One instant he was resisting, body shaking and convulsing, the next he was frozen, then limp, then nothing but a sack of flesh on the floor.

Master Shen was no more.

My ladies rushed to me as my legs gave way, supporting me, calling to me... and we glowed. I felt Cheri hold me to her breast, calling on me to take her, and I thought how absurd that thought was— that we should fuck right then and there, after all that. My head cleared more and I realized that, no, she was saying to take her energy, to replenish myself, and I remembered that I could heal, in a mental sense, and as all three held me, their energy flowed into me so that my legs had strength again and my mind returned to full awareness.

Then they were kissing me and laughing, and I, too, was exuberant—until the place started falling around us, explosions giving us warning that it was all falling apart. In taking Master Shen and the station core out, we'd doomed this place as we'd hoped we would.

Now we just had to find a way out of there.

20

"The shipyard," Tink said, reducing down to fairy-size again and fluttering about, pulling back as an explosion came too close for comfort. "That drill machine, I think it might work."

"It's our only option," I replied, and we ran for it, watching on the map as new walls formed and old ones blew apart. Meanwhile, heat signatures appeared on the map showing where fires were now raging and explosions going off. But I could see a pattern in it all, like the rotations of this place. I timed it, leading them along the routes we could find, new centers of gravity forming and throwing us against walls that became floors.

"We'll never make it like this," Erupa shouted.

"That doesn't mean we can stop trying," I replied,

charging around a falling wall, then pulling back and swearing as an explosion sent a burst of debris our way.

"Can't you shadow through?" Tink asked Erupa.

"Doesn't work that way—I need a person to focus on," Erupa replied, grabbing a portion of a wall that was in our way and bending it back.

Tink flew through but came back a second later. "Blocked!"

We turned back, sprinting through a hallway and then working to get between two collapsed walls, both with metal crunched in on us like a tin can that'd been stomped on. The way was almost clear, all of us charging on when another explosion hit overhead rocking the fabric of the tunnel, and the ceiling started to collapse. We turned back, but another explosion hit so now the floor fell out and we were sliding.

My legs hit the far wall, and I grabbed Erupa's hand, she Cheri's.

"In here," Tink called at the mouth of an opening. Cheri climbed up over us, the first through, and then I heaved Erupa up and in. She pulled me after her, and we sat there, catching our breaths while Tink checked the way ahead and I looked at it on the map.

"The station core room," I said. "It's the only area not changing, not exploding."

"Might be a safety option," Erupa said. "Get in and wait it out?"

"Or get in and bust our way out," Cheri said with an excited laugh. "Lilly tells me she saw some sort of control panels in the walls, so... Oh, and the other voices say yeah, that's the best option. Let's go."

She stood, turned, turned back again and frowned. "Big ol' balls, they don't know the way."

"I got it," I said, then called out for Tink. "We're going back to the station core room."

"Good," she said, fluttering back. "Because this way takes us there, but the other routes are blocked."

"Decision confirmed."

Another explosion rattled the walls, but we were up and moving, sliding down the passage as it started to move, and then we ran along the next, jumping into the inner section that seemingly wasn't impacted by the rest.

"Where, Cheri?" I asked, running around the inner room, looking for any sign of what she had been talking about. The walls had all manner of wires and odd box shapes sticking out, all metal, and lines and areas that could be hidden compartments, but Cheri walked right up to one, moved a few cables out of the way and then selected several metal knobs, turned them, and pressed in on one of those boxes.

Those voices of hers could be damn helpful.

To my delight, this wasn't so different from the ship I'd flown my delivery in on. Likely Orion Corp.-made, using the same basic programs and machinery. It didn't take long to figure out what was what. I selected the option to close all hatches, and then the outer parts were secure, a display appearing where a wall had been, controls moving out to me and seats rising up.

"This is fucking awesome!" Cheri shouted.

"I gotta agree," Tink said, fluttering around and laughing. "Holy shit, this is fun!"

"Fun?" I laughed. "You all are nuts."

Cheri just gave me a look this time, and I nodded. She didn't have to say it.

With me at the controls, we turned on shields and began tearing through walls, blasting out those we could and using the attached turning walls like drills, the alien metal stronger than anything the planet was made from.

It was insane, but as we went I found that I could maneuver the controls to shape this place so that it wasn't just a maze like when we'd gone in. This whole place could be maneuvered like a massive puzzle, and we were riding the controls. Soon I had an opening for us and we were pushing up past the surface, leaving explosions in our wake.

"Holy shit!" I shouted as we neared the surface and saw only darkness ahead, but then we were bursting through and it was just the night sky, and we were up into the open.

"Master Shen," a voice said, a face appearing at the edge of my display. "What is the meaning of..." The face, a woman with hair tied back and wearing an Orion Corp. military uniform, saw me then and glared. "There seems to be some confusion. You are not Master Shen."

"No, I'm not," I said. "And whoever you are, I'm coming for you. We're coming for you... all of you."

The lady cursed and the connection ceased but Erupa was there at my side, grinning. "It shows where the call came from."

"Are we really doing it?" Cheri asked, then bit her lip in excitement. "Are we really charging off to wage war on the entire Orion Corp. military? I fucking love it, I love it! It's so... psycho!"

I laughed. "Not alone. But with them, maybe." We had just turned the ship to see the planet below, and what looked like the end of a battle, the screen selecting various groups and zooming in, showing us all sorts of monsters from below, along with Trunk and his team and Letha and her two guys.

"Woohooo!" Tink shouted, growing to her full-size version again and wrapping her arms around me, pumping a fist in the air. "We've got a fucking war!"

"Fucking war, fucking war!" Cheri shouted, jumping up and down. "Wait, how's a fucking war work?"

"As in, we fuck on our way to war?" Tink said with a wink, then shrugged. "Maybe..."

Oh, shit, the way she looked at me with that *maybe* turned me on. If we were going to ride off to our possible deaths, taking as many of the Orion Corp. bastards with us as we could, we might as well get some action first and then go out in style.

But first, we had an army to pick up. As we grew closer, we saw that the other ships had arrived and been taken over, and Letha was calling through the comms that we needed to stand down or she'd shoot us out of the sky.

"It's us," I quickly replied, and then specified, "Ezra, the team you met below."

"No shit?" she asked. "About time you joined the fight. We took care of it all for you, don't worry."

I laughed. "We did our part down there, and will be happy to share our story if you share yours, once we're off this damn planet for good."

"Agreed," she said, and directed us where to land.

We touched down and cautiously exited, but Letha and Trunk were there, guard rifles in hand.

The fighting was over, their army of hybrids and various monsters waiting.

"Go time," Letha said. "We hacked the ships, got a few former guards on our side. I'm making a move against Orion Corp. Are you with me?"

"You bet your fucking ass we are!" Cheri said, hanging off of me.

I grabbed Cheri around the waist, snarled playfully, and then looked up at Letha. "Means yes."

"Damn straight," Letha said, watching us with excitement. "I like your style. What do I call you?"

"The Psychobitches," I replied.

Letha approached, gesturing out at the crowd. "This will be our victory. This is our chance... but also the other group I mentioned? The one with the woman who had fox ears and a tail? They left a message for us. See here."

She took a comms unit from one of the ships and opened a message. There was a man looking out of the screen, the fox lady with her pink hair and others behind him too—one with green hair, another with blue skin but in a less demonic way than Erupa. (For the record, I preferred the wild Erupa look, but could see how this man would be into this one. Everyone has their own tastes).

"Survivors of Abaddon," the man said. "I am called Breaker, though I am originally an Earther named Chad. We are in pursuit of Muerta and mean to take her and the entire Orion Corp. down, followed by all others who stand on the side of evil. If you are listening, that means you were victorious this day, and I hope you are on the side of justice. Join me, if you will—rise up! We've taken the liberty of fixing the spacecraft there so that you might fly out to join us in our assault. When it's over, I have much to tell you about your world and another, and about a place called the Citadel where you will be welcome. I look forward to that day, but first... off to war. We'll see you there."

"I recognize some of them," Erupa said, still staring at the device as the window closed. "Twitch, for one... she was thrown in prison for destroying a whole planet when she was supposed to be defending it. Gale for betraying the Citadel. I don't understand."

"You don't believe people can change their ways?" I asked her. "Second chances and all that?"

She looked into my eyes and said, "I do."

"Then we join them. Letha, may I?" At her nod, I turned and motioned to the army. "Everyone, prepare to embark! It's time to teach those motherfuckers at Orion Corp. that they don't mess with us!"

A cheer rose up in response, and then Letha put her fist in the air and shouted, "Kill 'em all!"

With that, everyone made for the ships. Letha and her team with a handful of others took one of the guard fighters, Trunk and his crew were in another, and we took on some hybrids and whatnot as well, including, I saw, one who looked an awful lot like the mermaid we'd seen, but with legs. I wondered if they could transform, but figured I'd find out soon enough.

Everyone boarded, we kicked the engines into gear and took off.

Destination: Orion Corp. military headquarters, we assumed.

Mission: Fuck and war. Probably in that order, and then fuck some more.

All of these ships behind us, at least two dozen, including our huge craft that had once been the station core of the planet, two large ships sent by Orion Corp. itself, and then the fighters. It wasn't a fleet, but it would hopefully be enough to raise hell. And somewhere out there, this man Breaker and his team were already leading the charge, likely taking the heat off of us as we rode up to join the battle.

Soon we were in open space, the ship on autopilot, and Tink fluttered over, reminding me that I was well overdue for some nourishment and rest. I completely agreed, leaving Erupa to watch over the ship and keep an eye out for trouble.

However, as I stumbled back, my eyes started closing, and I figured food could come after rest. I found a back room made up for sleep. Judging by the ancient weapons and even an image of the temple, it had to have been a room Master Shen used. *Mine now, motherfucker,* I thought as I stripped, collapsed into the bed, and curled up on my side, passing out.

My dreams were blissful mornings on the beach, watching the sunrise. There I was, on the orange and pink beach with Cheri, Erupa, and Tink (in full form), wading into the waters, nude, laughing. The water reached my groin and tickled, and then it wasn't water at all, but their tongues and lips, and I craved the taste of all of them at once.

Sleep slowly left and my eyelids fluttered open. I let out a soft moan, seeing the metal ceiling above and realizing the sensation hadn't finished, that I was still in this state of bliss, and that I had massive morning wood.

I felt a tingling sensation run up my spine and looked down to see movement under the sheets. It scared me, but then another flash of pleasure took hold and I bit my lip to keep from moaning loudly. Lifting up the sheet, my eyes went wide at what I saw.

There was Tink, fluttering around my hard cock, her wings tickling me, her hands caressing the curves. Seeing me awake, she grinned and said, "They wanted me to wake you up. Figured you might like it this way."

I nodded, not sure how to answer, and she grinned. "Close your eyes, let me finish."

"Damn, I love being a Psychobitch," I said as I lay back and let her keep having her fun. A quote I'd once heard played in my head, though the exact words escaped me. Some Earther saying, I thought. All I knew was that, whatever tomorrow brought, I was happy to let it do its worst because I had lived today.

ABOUT THE AUTHOR

Jamie Hawke

After working on Marvel properties and traveling the world, Jamie Hawke decided to settle down and write fun, quirky, and sexy pulp science fiction and superhero books. Are they all harem? Oh yeah. Oh yeahhhh.

It all started when Jamie was eleven, creating nude superhero comics with his best friend. What perverts! But hey, they were fun and provided good fodder for jokes up into their adult years. Now the stories have evolved, but they capture that same level of fun. Hopefully you will enjoy them as much as the author loved writing them!

* * *

All caught up on Jamie Hawke books? If you like Gamelit (with a lite harem setup) check out KILL CODE.

AUTHOR RAMBLINGS

This has been your latest installment in the Supers universe - hope you enjoyed it! I'm kind of calling this book the unofficial Ex Heroes 3.5, but it's also connected to Planet Kill (where Letha was one of the Point of View characters). If you haven't read all of those books, please do! Keep on reading for links.

I had some fun titling this book, though one friend didn't want me to go with Psychobitches at first. When he later saw that it was more about owning it and empowerment, he sang a different tune.

But where did it start? Naturally, with my twelve-year old self reading Tank Girl comics. Then there were others, like Harley Quinn and the one from

League of Legends... oh, and Tiny Tina (Borderlands - I was lucky enough to work on a Borderlands game at Telltale as a writer, so did a lot of playing those original games and loved the Tiny Tina story). As you can see, I'm a big fan of the story of these people who are a bit outlandish, so wanted to capture that to the extreme in this book. I also had feedback talking about my crazy people in the Ex Heroes books, and thought that I could one-up those as far as levels of craziness.

What do you think? Mission successful?

As for next books, I hope to do a sequel here, as long as you all want me too. We'll also see some of these characters (Letha included) in the next Ex Heroes books, so stay tuned for that. I'm continuing to jot down new ideas for Harem Gamelit books, and will keep seeing what excites me at the moment. I'm writing these for fun, so if I take a little bit to get to the next one, please be patient and read all the rest of the books in the meantime.

Can I ask a favor? If you enjoyed this book, please go leave a review. They really do help. It's also kind of a way of voting for which book comes next, so the more love you show, the sooner another book will come.

I also love hearing from you all! Find my Facebook group and join me in chatting about this story and others. What did you like most? What didn't work for you? Let's discuss.

Thank you again for reading!

Jamie Hawke

I'm super excited and hope you'll follow me on Facebook and Amazon (Click here and then 'Follow' under my name/pic). That way, you won't miss it! It's probably my best work ever.

Thank you again, and I look forward to hearing from you!

To connect directly:

https://www.facebook.com/groups/JamieHawke/

Also, for my GameLit Harem newsletter:

http://bit.ly/HaremGamelit

Do you want more Harem? I recommend this
Facebook Group:

HaremGamelit Group

READ NEXT

Thank you for reading this book! Please consider laving a review on Amazon and Goodreads. And don't miss out on the newsletter:

SIGN UP HERE

***

Don't miss the bestseller SUPERS: EX HEROES.

Super powers. Super harem. Super awesome.

Contains Adult Content. Seriously.

Who in their right mind tells both his lawyer and the judge presiding over his murder trial, "Fuck you!" while still in the courtroom? No one, right? Yeah, you'd be wrong about that. I did.

You'd say the same thing if you were just found guilty of a murder you didn't commit, though. Call me crazy for going off like that in court, but trust me, you don't know crazy until you see what happened next.

I never believed in superheroes. I certainly didn't believe that I'd become one, or that strategically forming a harem of hot chicas and getting down with them to unlock my superpowers would be the key to my survival.

Did I say my survival? I meant the universe's. No, really...that's exactly what happened when I was taken to a galaxy of supers, thrown into a prison ship full of villains, and told it was up to me to stop them all.

Read on, friend, because it gets a whole hell of a lot crazier from here.

***

Want something a bit more insane? Planet Kill is like Battle Royale on a planet with Gamelit elements... and it's crazy. You'll see - You can grab book one and two on Amazon!

Grab PLANET KILL now!

Form your harem. Kill or be killed. Level up and loot. Welcome to Planet Kill.

Pierce has his mission: survive by killing and getting nasty, doing whatever it takes to find his lost wife and others who were abducted and forced to participate in the barbarity that is Planet Kill. In a galaxy where the only way to rise up in society and make it to the paradise planets is through this insanity, he will be up against the most desperate, the most ruthless, and the sexiest fighters alive.

Because it's not just a planet--it's the highest rated show around. Contestants level up for kills, get paid for accepting violent and sexual bids, and factions have been made in the form of harems.

His plan starts to come together when he meets Letha, one of the most experienced warlords on the planet. She's as lethal as they come and a thousand times as sexy. He's able to learn under her, to start to form his own harem.

Only, being her ally means fighting her wars.

It's kill or be killed, level up fast and put on the show the viewers want all while proving to Letha and her generals that he has what it takes to be one of them. The alternative is death, leaving his wife to her fate of being hunted by monsters.